THE
MERLIN EFFECT

THE
MERLIN EFFECT

T. A. BARRON

PHILOMEL BOOKS ♦ NEW YORK

Copyright © 1994 by Thomas A. Barron
Illustrations copyright © 1994 by Anthony Bacon Venti
All rights reserved. This book, or parts thereof, may not be reproduced in any form
without permission in writing from the publisher. Philomel Books, a division of
Penguin Putnam Books for Young Readers, 345 Hudson Street, New York, NY 10014.
Philomel Books, Reg. U.S. Pat. & Tm. Off. Published simultaneously in Canada.
Book design by Gunta Alexander. Text set in Caslon.
Library of Congress Cataloging-in-Publication Data
Barron, T. A. The Merlin effect / by T. A. Barron. p. cm.
Summary: When she joins her father and several others investigating a strange
whirlpool and possible sunken treasure ship off the coast of Baja California,
thirteen-year-old Kate is drawn into a centuries-old conflict between Merlin
and the evil Nimue. 1. Merlin (Legendary character)—Juvenile Fiction
[1. Merlin (Legendary character)—Fiction.   2. Buried treasure—Fiction.
3. Fathers and daughters—Fiction.] I Title. ISBN 0-399-22689-3
PZ7.B27567Me   1994   [Fic]—dc20   93-36234 CIP AC
10 9 8

To my father,
ARCH BARRON

With special appreciation to
BROOKS,
age four, who will one day sing with the whales
and to
TERRY,
who values the empty places between stars
as well as the stars themselves

Thanks also to those who advised me on matters of science: Eric,
on genetics; Charlie, on whirlpools; Celia, on marine flora and
fauna; and a certain gray whale off Baja California, who swam
up to my kayak and let me touch his back.

The whirlpool drowned the treasure ship
Upon that dreadful morn,
And buried it beneath the waves
Along with Merlin's Horn.

And so today the ship's at rest,
Removed from ocean gales,
Surrounded by a circle strange
Of ever-singing whales.

A prophesy clings to the ship
Like barnacles to wood.
Its origins remain unknown,
Its words not understood:

One day the sun will fail to rise,
The dead will die,
    And then
For Merlin's Horn to find its home,
The ship must sail again.

—fragments from
"The Ballad of the *Resurrección*"

IN SEARCH OF THE LOST SHIP
RESURRECCÍON AND THE
MERLIN EFFECT
The Lost Realm of Shaa
The Glass House
Monsters of the Deep
The Resurreccion
(Wrecked 1547 A.D.)
The ever singing whales

One day the sun will fail to rise
The dead will die . . . and then
For Merlin's Horn to find its home
The ship must sail again.

A.B.VENTI

N

Fishing
Village

Research
Station

Second
buoy

the
Last dune

San
Lazaro
Lagoon

Breakers

Baja
California
MEXICO

The Whirlpool
Remolino de la Muerté

-PACIFIC
OCEAN-

The Skimmer
towing the submersible

Mer People

Pieces of eight

CONTENTS

PART ONE:
BEYOND THE LAGOON

1

At Sea

Farther from shore, nearer to death.

With every pull of her paddle, Kate recalled the much-repeated warning about these waters. Yet today felt different. Today the sea looked tranquil, even inviting.

Her arms, brown after almost a month in the Baja California sun, churned rhythmically. The kayak cut through the water, slicing the glassy green walls that rose and fell like a heaving chest. As the protected lagoon receded behind her, open ocean stretched before her. The swollen sun drifted low on the horizon, glowing like a lump of melting gold.

A wave slapped the kayak, drenching her. She shook herself, pulled a piece of kelp off her forearm, then resumed paddling.

She glided past the forest of mangroves lining the mouth of the lagoon. Despite the low tide, she skirted within a few feet of their long, spindly roots. Planted in the mud, they resembled a family of long-legged waders. An immature heron resting on a branch watched her slide by, but Kate's attention had turned to a copper-stained mound at the end of the bay. The last dune. And beyond it, the breakers.

Never been out this far before, she thought. What a place to see the sunset! Too bad she had waited so long to venture out. Now only a few more days remained before she would have to leave all this for good.

She lay the paddle across her lap, licking the salt from her sunburned lips. As the vessel coasted quietly with the current, she listened to the trickle of water running down the ends of the paddle. Slowly, the sun ignited sea and sky with streaks of crimson. Just beneath the waves, a web of golden light shimmered.

A plover swooped past, barely a foot above her head, searching for a crab-meat supper. Meanwhile, two sandpipers, standing one legged in the shadow of the dune, chittered noisily next to the hissing, rushing waves. Kate drew in a deep breath, feeling the warmth of the fading sun on her face. At midday, it had struck with brutal force, yet now it soothed like a gentle massage.

As the current pulled her past the last dune, she scanned the line of whitecaps ahead. The breakers splashed and sucked, a stark barrier of volcanic rock. Yet the ocean beyond looked calm, serene, almost deserving of the name Pacific. At this moment, it was hard to believe all those tales of sudden squalls, murderous shoals, and swelling tides that had made this stretch of Mexican coast a sailor's nightmare for centuries. Not to mention the legendary *Remolino de la Muerté,* the Whirlpool of Death, discussed by the local people only in whispers.

True or not, those tales—along with the harshness of the desert landscape—had kept the population of this area to a few scattered fishing villages. Almost nobody came here by choice. That is, until her father plunked his research team at San Lazaro Lagoon.

With a flick of her paddle, she spun the kayak around to face the lagoon. At the far end sat the research camp, its white canvas tents washed in the rich colors of sunset. Behind them rose the flagpole, still sporting the purple T-shirt hoisted by her father when the official colors blew away, and the wind generator, its steel propeller spinning lazily. Close to the beach, the converted trawler *Skimmer* lay anchored. Not far away bobbed the silver-colored submersible, awaiting its next deep-water dive.

She shook her head. Dad was still working on the boat. Though she could not see him, she could hear the familiar sputtering of the aging trawler's engine. It didn't make any difference that the ship was almost beyond repair, that the project's days were numbered, or that a spectacular sunset was about to happen. He probably wouldn't budge to see a sea monster taking a bubble bath in the lagoon. Or the lost ship *Resurrección*, laden with treasure, rising out of the waves as the old legend predicted.

And the others on his team were no better. Terry constantly fiddled with his scientific equipment, whether in his tent, on the *Skimmer*, or on the team's two buoys. Isabella, for her part, divided her time between her makeshift laboratory and the submersible, which she pampered as if it were her own baby. She would be down inside its hatch right now, doing her evening maintenance, if she had not agreed yesterday to work the camp's radio constantly in a last-ditch attempt to get the project's permit extended.

During the past few weeks, Kate's job as cook and dishwasher for the team had allowed her plenty of time for exploring the beach, snorkeling, scaling dunes, or taking sunset kayak rides. None of the others had ever joined her, not even her father. So much for her high hopes of spending lots of time with him in this isolated lagoon. She had seen only a little more of him than she had of her mother, who was thousands of miles away at their home in New England.

For a while, she had at least been able to share supper with him when the group assembled in the main tent at the end of each day. Lately, though, even that tradition had suffered, as everyone worked later and later into the night. The specter of the project's permit expiring, with no results to show for the entire month, hung like a dark cloud over them. Especially her father. He had given up trying to learn anything useful from the villagers, and had spent the last twenty-four hours on the *Skimmer,* trying to adapt Terry's precious equipment to his own purposes. Outside of his increasingly tense arguments with Terry, his conversations had shrunk to a distracted *thank-you* to Kate whenever she brought him some food.

Not that this so-called team had much in common to talk about anyway. Isabella was a marine biologist, Terry a graduate student in undersea geology, Kate's father a historian. He was leader of the group in name only. About the only thing they managed to do cooperatively was to tow the submersible out to sea for Isabella's deep-water dives.

Kate dipped her paddle and heaved. The kayak spun like a leaf on the water. Once more she was facing the sinking sun. Its color had gone from gold to crimson, and it seemed squashed, as if a great boot were stepping on it.

With a start, she realized she had drifted out and was almost on top of the breakers. Rough water boiled just ahead. Quickly, she paddled a few furious strokes in reverse, then started to turn the craft around. Better to watch the sunset from inside the lagoon. That way she would be sure to get back in plenty of time to prepare supper.

Suddenly she halted. The breakers didn't really look so

bad. Not nearly as dangerous as the rapids at Devil's Canyon where she had kayaked last summer. Sure, Dad had firmly cautioned her never to cross them. Yet he and Terry did it every day in the *Skimmer* to check the buoys. The white water would make a thrilling ride. She might not get another chance. And besides, she was thirteen now, old enough to make her own decisions.

Surveying the line of turbulence, she picked the best point to cross. Farther out, in the calmer waters of the sea, the team's two buoys floated, decorated with brightly colored equipment. The first buoy seemed surprisingly close; the second, much farther out. In the distance, beyond the second buoy, a spiraling tower of mist hovered over the sea, swirling slowly. For an instant, the mist thinned just enough to reveal an ominous pursing of the waves, rising out of the water like an undersea volcano.

Farther from shore, nearer to . . .

Kate bit her lip. It was probably nothing more than a reef. And even if it were something more dangerous, it was too far away to pose any risk. Whatever, it seemed to taunt her, daring her to cross the breakers.

She glanced over her shoulder at the research camp. No one would miss her. Absorbed as he was, her father wouldn't even notice if supper came a little late tonight.

Just as she raised her paddle, a lone gull screeched overhead. She hesitated, looked again out to sea. The distant mist had thickened once more, concealing whatever she had seen. Sucking in her breath, she propelled herself at the breakers.

The wind gusted slightly, playing with her braid, as she drove the kayak forward. Effortless as a frigate bird soaring on the swells, she raced across the water.

"Hooeeee!" she shouted aloud as the craft plunged into the

whitecaps. She paddled even faster. The narrow boat almost seemed to lift above the waves.

With a final splash, she cleared the breakers completely. The water grew calm again. Breathing hard, she placed the paddle across her lap and glided toward the sunset.

It was nearly time. Rays of peach and purple mingled with the sky's brighter flames. The rippling crests around her quivered with scarlet light. Water birds fell silent. The sun pressed lower and lower, flattening against the sea. Then, in the blink of an eye, it dropped below the horizon.

She shifted her gaze to the strange spiral of mist beyond the second buoy. Was it only her imagination, or could she hear a distant humming sound from that direction?

Absently, she drummed the shaft of the paddle. A trick of the ocean air, perhaps? The local villagers claimed to have seen and heard many bizarre things off this coast. Isabella, who had grown up not far from here, had told Kate many of their tales during lulls in her lab work.

Too many, probably. One night last week, while paddling in the lagoon, Kate had heard what sounded like wispy voices, wailing and moaning in the distance. What was she to think? That she had heard the ghosts of the *Resurrección*'s sailors, swallowed by the whirlpool nearly five centuries ago? She was too embarrassed to tell anyone about it, or about how poorly she had slept that night. She was too old for that kind of thing.

Yet . . . her father didn't seem to be. He had spent his whole career as a historian trying to prove that some pretty far-fetched stories could actually be true.

Jim Gordon had a reputation as an accessible man, one of the most approachable people at the university. People rarely bothered to call him professor. Just Jim would do. No matter that he was one of the world's leading scholars on the legend of King Arthur, that he had done more than anyone to prove that Merlin was not merely a fictional wizard but a real person, a Druid prophet who lived long ago in what is now Wales. His book *The Life of Merlin* had become not only a classic study of the links between myth and history but a popular best-seller as well.

Many, including Kate, wondered why a Spanish galleon wrecked off Baja California should be of any interest to him, a professor of early English history. But on that subject, he kept silent. Even to his colleagues. Even to his daughter.

Kate slapped the water angrily with her paddle. Jim this. Jim that. If he were so approachable, how come she found it so hard to get any time with him? Something had happened to the father she used to know, the father who used to enjoy nothing more than leaning back in his chair and telling a good story about ancient heroes and gallant quests.

A briny breeze blew over the water. Feeling a bit chilly, she reached under the kayak's spray skirt and took out a crumpled blue cotton shirt. As she unsnapped her life jacket to slip into the shirt, she looked back toward the camp. A band of pink shone in the sky above the tents. Although it was still light, a sprinkling of stars had started to appear overhead.

Then she saw the moon, rising out of the eastern horizon like an evening sun. At first only a wispy halo lifted above the desert hills, then a slice of gold, then a disc of dazzling orange. Higher the moon rose, climbing slowly into the twilight sky. It cast a fiery path across the water, a path that burned its way to her tiny vessel, flooding her with amber light.

Turning again out to sea, she followed the rippled path to

the buoys and beyond. The waves glittered, as if paved with gold.

She took up her paddle. There was just enough time, if she hurried, for a brief sprint to the first buoy before dark. Kitchen duty could wait for once. She grinned, picturing the amazed look on her father's face when she would tell him what she had done.

She began to paddle toward the open ocean.

II

DARKNESS

Vigorously she stroked. The kayak surged forward, bounding over the water. Even as the sky darkened overhead, the full moon brightened, lighting her way.

She raced toward the first buoy, her heart pounding more from exhilaration than from exertion. Only twenty more strokes and she would be there. A gust of wind pushed the kayak slightly off course, but with a hard pull to starboard she corrected it. Fifteen, twelve, ten. She raced a gull, skimming the waves. Five more. Three more.

Her wake washed against the first buoy. She exhaled in satisfaction and set down her paddle. From this close, she could see the full extent of the buoy's gadgetry. Cylinders, plastic cases and colorful cables dangled from its sides. Thick nylon netting covered most of its base, shielding it from dolphins and other curious marine life. Its gleaming transmitter dish, aimed toward shore, gave it the appearance of a refugee robot from space.

Coming about, she wiped the perspiration from her brow with the sleeve of her shirt. Darkness was settling, but the camp remained visible among the dunes. Someone had switched on a light.

She glanced to the rear. The tower of mist beyond the second buoy seemed anything but threatening now, a billowy presence curling on the waves.

Then she heard the humming. The same sound she had heard before, only louder. It came from somewhere out to sea, somewhere behind the mist. Like the drone of a distant engine, it churned steadily, ceaselessly.

She tried to pinpoint its source but could see nothing. A boat out there? Unlikely. The *Skimmer* was back at camp. Fishermen didn't stay out this late. Who else might be sailing after sunset? That was a good way to end up like the *Resurrección*, dragged down by . . .

The whirlpool! So that's what that was. *Remolino de la Muerté*, considered by some to be as ancient and foreboding as the sea itself. She shivered slightly. Perhaps the sailors on board the *Resurrección* had heard that very same humming, only to drown a few moments later.

Raising her paddle, she turned back to shore. Airy fingers of fog were spreading across the lagoon. With any luck, she would return to camp with a little light to spare.

Just as she dipped her paddle in the water, another sound arrested her. At first she thought it was the kayak, creaking strangely. Then she realized it was more of a banging sound, coming from behind her.

She swung her head back out to sea, straining to hear. Although it was hard to tell, the new sound seemed disconnected from the constant humming of the whirlpool, and closer. Between the rhythmic pulsing of the waves against her boat, it banged irregularly, like an off-key bell. Now it beat furiously, now it died away, now it came back again.

Something about this sound gave Kate the eerie feeling that it came from a living creature. Like a person drowning, flailing, fighting for another breath. Yet she knew well the ocean often distorted sounds. It could be nothing more than the waves pummeling a reef.

A sudden motion caught her eye and she focused on the second buoy, perhaps a hundred yards away. A large object, silver in the moonlight, rose out of the waves and smacked the buoy with terrific force. The buoy rocked violently, almost toppling over. Something was trapped there!

She turned again toward shore. Whether from thickening fog or deepening darkness, the tents could now barely be seen. Another light went on, flickering weakly. She had to start back.

Then a high-pitched shriek ripped the air, lowering to a piteous wail. It came from the second buoy. She had no idea what kind of creature could make such a sound. She only knew it was a creature in pain.

Biting her lip, she whirled the kayak around. Her paddle spun in the air as she raced toward the far buoy. Salty spray stung her eyes, but she covered the distance in seconds.

As she approached, a hulking body lifted slightly above the waves and took an exhausted gasp of air before thrashing and rolling wildly in the water. A new wave drenched her, and with it came recognition. It was a whale.

Never had Kate seen a living being so large, at least three or four times her height in length. White barnacles peppered the whale's glistening skin, covering head, back and fins.

Isabella had mentioned that a small group of gray whales remained near the lagoon all year round, instead of joining the rest of their kind in the annual migration to the Arctic. Although this behavior baffled scientists, no one had ever succeeded in getting close enough to study them. All anyone knew was that the whales stayed by the whirlpool, circling and singing without rest.

Isabella had even given Kate a brief lesson in whale biology in case she should be lucky enough to see one of them during her kayak trips. She had only half listened, estimating her chances of spotting a whale at zero. Yet there could be no mistaking this huge creature that was right here before her, struggling to stay alive.

Careful to keep clear of the enormous body, Kate brought her kayak nearer to the buoy. She realized, as the whale rolled over, that she had encountered a young male. Big as he was, he had only reached half of his adult size. If, in fact, he ever made it to adulthood. For his plight was clear. His tail flukes were completely tangled in the nylon net attached to the buoy. Wires wrapped tightly, sliced deeply. Blood swirled on the water. The corner of one fluke hung loose, nearly severed.

Once more the whale flailed, knocking his tail against the instruments, blowing a blast of spray that rained down on Kate. She stowed her paddle and leaned over to the side, nearly swamping the kayak, trying to pull the net off the tail, itself almost as big as her boat. Yet as hard as she tugged, the net would not come free.

Bracing her hands on the slippery skin, she tried again, pulling with all her strength. No success.

Her fingers stiff from cold, she reached for one of the two big knots attaching the net to the buoy. At length she succeeded in untying it. Carefully, she pulled herself over to the other knot. It resisted, but finally gave way. As the net slid into the water, she felt a surge of hope. Then she realized that the net connected to the buoy in a third place, at the base of the transmitter dish.

At that instant, the great tail whipped out of the waves, smacking her hard across her left side. The kayak flipped over, plunging her into icy blackness. She swallowed water, struggling to breathe. Her arms flailed, but she could not pull herself out of the boat. Pain shot through her chest, throbbed in her head. Desperately, she punched at her spray skirt to free herself.

Suddenly she tasted air again. She gagged, coughing up sea water. The momentum of her roll had flipped the kayak upright, but the boat now rode dangerously low. Her sun hat was gone; her spray skirt was torn. Choking, she rubbed her stinging eyes, as water cascaded down from her hair and shoulders.

Even as she scolded herself for trying to rescue a whale all by herself, the injured animal abruptly ceased fighting. But for a single quivering fin, he lay motionless in the water.

She surveyed the young leviathan, lying limp by the buoy. Resignedly, she looked toward shore. The wavering lights of camp seemed to welcome her, offering warmth and safety and dry land. Then the whale stirred, releasing a low, shivery moan, the sound of a living being preparing to die.

The whale's eye, as round and silver as the moon itself, met hers. For a long moment, they held each other's gaze.

Instinctively, she reached for the transmitter dish where the nylon net connected to the buoy. One of the two rods anchoring the dish to the buoy had already broken. Perhaps . . . She stretched herself farther, farther, waves slapping against the boat and her chest, until at last her hand grasped the remaining rod.

She hesitated. This equipment belonged to the team. Her father, she knew, was trying to use it, as was Terry. Breaking off the dish might cause some real damage.

Once more she peered into the silver eye. It watched her intently, not blinking.

Clenching her teeth, she gave a wrenching tug. The rod snapped, the transmitter dish plunged into the water.

Several seconds passed. The whale did not move. Then, suddenly, his tail lifted, yanking the net free from the buoy. His massive head bent downward. His flukes, red with blood, arched upward before smacking the water with such force that Kate nearly capsized from the wave. Then he dived into the depths, pulling behind the transmitter dish ensnared in a web of nylon.

Alone again, she retrieved her paddle. Spotting a flickering light through the mist, she started for shore, feeling exhausted but pleased with herself. Water sloshed inside the kayak, but she could do nothing about that now. A loose object bumped into her leg: her father's headlamp, stored in the kayak for evening outings. Strapping it on her forehead, she flicked it on, sending a thin white beam across the bow.

A big wave tumbled over her, soaking her again. Then another. She paddled hard, ignoring the growing ache between her shoulder blades. For some reason, the going seemed more difficult this direction. A tricky bit of current, perhaps, or the added weight of the water she had taken on. Her arms felt weaker with every stroke. Her head hummed.

At once, she realized the humming was not just in her head. Checking over her shoulder, she saw rising out of the mist a great bulge of water, coursing and crashing under the lamplike moon.

The whirlpool! The current had dragged her closer! She threw all her effort into every pull of her paddle. But *Remolino de la Muerté* tugged steadily at her slender craft. Her shoulders throbbed. As she grew more tired, the boat began to slip backward. In no time, she lost what little headway she had gained. Soon the second buoy disappeared into fog.

Again she stole a glance to the rear. Now the whirlpool jutted out of the sea like a circular tsunami. Spiraling whitecaps curled around its frothy rim, climbing steadily toward the center. Sheets of cold spray rained down on her.

Terror crowded out her thoughts, growing with the din of the whirlpool. She stroked feverishly, though waves battered the boat and she could no longer see the lights of the camp. Even the moon faded now and then from view, obscured by the rising spray.

Then, not far ahead, a dark shadow appeared. Slowly, against the swirling mist, the form grew fuller and sharper. Broad at the base and ragged at the top, it lifted above the water as precipitously as an island. But Kate, catching her breath, knew it was no island.

It was a ship.

Suddenly, a great wave swept over her, an avalanche of foam, capsizing the kayak. A few seconds later, the small boat drifted back to the surface, floating aimlessly. For now it carried no passenger.

III

THE HORN OF MERLIN

Scrambled eggs, coming up," announced Jim Gordon, trying for the third time to light the burner. "Just got to get this blasted thing to work. Meanwhile, you can finish off that tea in my thermos."

He struck another match, then blew gently on the gas outlet while holding the flame as close as possible. With a *whooosh*, the burner caught fire, just as the match started to singe his fingers.

"Ow! There now. We're set." He straightened his tall, lanky frame, so that his bristly brown hair grazed the ceiling of the boat's cabin. Planting a heavy cast-iron pan on the sputtering burner, he tossed in a lump of butter. As the smell of sizzling butter filled the cabin, he wiped the mist inside the window with his sleeve, scanned the dark waters outside, then observed the girl in the corner bundled under two wool blankets. Beside her on the floor lay her wet clothes in a pile.

Kate raised her head, looked into his chocolate brown eyes. "Pretty stupid, huh?" She took a sip from the mug in her hands.

Her father cocked his head and started cracking eggs into

the pan. "No, I wouldn't say stupid. More like idiotic." He threw the shells into a trash bin under the steering wheel. "That was a close call for both of us. I try hard never to go out past the second buoy."

She listened to the waves lapping at the sides of the *Skimmer*. "I can see why."

"At least you had enough sense to wear your life jacket. And that headlamp. I never would have seen you otherwise."

"It was dumb luck, not sense."

Turning back to the eggs, Jim began stirring them with an old wooden spoon. "Like them plain? Or my special way, Baja Scramble?"

"Your way is fine," mumbled Kate feebly. She swallowed some more tea, her eyes roaming the boat's interior. The chipping gray paint, the shelves of food supplies, the boxes of diving equipment and spare parts, and the piles of nautical maps gave no hint that this was anything but a normal shrimp trawler. Only the counter by the burner, piled high with computer equipment, discarded printouts, and reference books on sonic imaging, revealed anything different.

"How come you were out so far in the kayak?"

"I was just, ah . . . exploring."

"Exploring!" Jim stopped stirring. "You could have been killed!"

She frowned, said nothing.

"Don't you know there's a whirlpool near here? Half a mile wide and probably just as deep?"

"Sure, but—"

"Then what ever possessed you to come out so far?"

"The second buoy." She paused, on the edge of describing her contact with the whale, then thought better of it. "I wanted to, ah, check it out."

Her father scrutinized her, then resumed cooking.

"You've got to respect the sea, Kate. It's full of surprises, often deadly. It's no place to play around. There's an old saying about this coastline. *Mas lejos de la orilla, mas cerca de la muerté.* It means *Farther from shore . . .*"

"*Nearer to death,*" she finished grimly. Trying to change the subject, she asked, "So why were you out with the *Skimmer?* You almost never sail after dark."

Jim tasted the eggs, then went back to stirring. "Well, it's like this. You know how long it's taken me to get Terry to part with his precious equipment so I could use it to take a sonic picture?"

"Ever since we got here."

"Right. Well, no sooner do I get it all set up and start to shoot the area right under the whirlpool than the screen goes blank. Completely blank! The monitor showed a malfunction at the second buoy, so I hustled out here to check."

Kate stiffened. "The second buoy?"

He glanced her way. "Don't worry, we're safe. I've got us tied up tight to the buoy. We'll only stay here a little while longer, so I can do the repairs."

Stirring uneasily, she asked, "Repairs?"

"On the sonar gear." Pouting, he wiped the spoon on the edge of the pan. "Some damned sea animal decided to get playful with the transmitter dish. Broke it clean off, though I'm sure it's still there, tangled up in the net someplace."

Again she stirred beneath the blankets. "What if the transmitter dish is . . . gone?"

"Sunk? No chance. I tied those knots myself."

"But—"

"Before I can repair the buoy, though, I need to see if any data got stored before the dish broke off." Reaching his long arm to the topmost shelf, he steadied himself against the rocking of the waves and pulled down a jar of salsa. As he unscrewed the cap, he nodded toward a black cable stretching from the computer out the door of the cabin. "I'm processing that right now. It'll take a few minutes. The equipment here on the boat isn't as powerful as what we have back at camp."

Pouring the spicy salsa into the pan, he mixed it with the eggs. "I'm glad you've learned your lesson. All my life I've been around water, and I've never seen anything half as dangerous as this coast. If I didn't have to come here to find out more about that galleon, believe me, I'd be somewhere else."

Feeling he just might be ready to open up to her, Kate decided to save the truth about the transmitter dish for later. She drew in her breath. "What's so special about that old ship, anyway?"

Dumping a heap of eggs on a plastic plate, he handed it to her. "There you go, Baja Scramble."

"Thanks," she replied, looking dubiously at the concoction. Suddenly, the aroma aroused her hunger. She took a small bite. "Hey, this is pretty good." Another bite followed, then another. "Can't believe how hungry I am."

"A swim will do that," he said wryly.

"Now can you tell me?"

He aimed a fork at the eggs in the pan. "Tell you what?"

"What's so special about that ship."

Glancing at his watch, he said, "Almost time to see what we've got. Then a few quick repairs and you'll be back at camp before you know it."

Kate surveyed the cabin, her head swaying to the rhythm of the waves. She sensed she should try a different approach. "Want to hear something crazy? When I first saw your boat, in all that mist, you'll never guess what I thought it was."

"Let me guess. The Navy? The *QE II?*"

"No," she answered. "Even crazier. I thought you were the sunken ship, sailing again like the legend says."

"The *Resurreccíon?*" Jim laughed. "Guess I've infected you with my own wild dreams." He grinned mysteriously. "You never know, though. Myth and reality aren't always so far apart."

"Something you've tried to show with Merlin."

"That's right," he said through a mouthful of eggs. "Merlin's life and legend are impossibly intertwined. That's one reason a lot of people still refuse to believe he was a real person."

Kate stabbed at the remains on her plate, then asked as casually as she could manage, "Will raising the *Resurreccíon* help you settle something about Merlin?"

"You could say that."

"But, Dad, we're in Mexico. Halfway around the world from where Merlin lived! What could he have to do with this place?"

"More than you know," he replied, setting down his fork. "But raising the old ship isn't really necessary. Besides, there's no way, with this little manpower and time, I could ever hope to do that. Especially with the whirlpool so near. All I need to do is prove the *Resurreccíon* actually existed. If I can just do that, then . . ."

"Then what?"

"Then I can organize a proper expedition to salvage whatever is left of it."

"Then what?"

Jim tugged playfully on her braid. "Then maybe you'll stop asking so many questions."

"I learned that from you."

"I see your point. Historians do ask questions for a living.

All right, then, here's one for you. How about some hot cocoa? I think there's some powdered milk around here someplace." He took a plastic container from the shelf and set it down with a thud. "Now all we need is the cocoa."

"Please tell me."

"All right. Tell you what?"

Straightening her back, she asked, "What could Merlin have to do with the ship? Besides, didn't he live in the fifth or sixth century? The *Resurrección* went down—"

"In 1547," completed her father. "You remember more of the old bedtime stories than I thought. Could it be you're a fan of Merlin, too?"

"I *hate* Merlin," blustered Kate, surprised at the force of her own words. "He's just a stupid magician. I couldn't care less about him. But if I listened to your Merlin stories, I got to see you every once in a while! At least that used to be true before you got all wrapped up with this ship project."

Jim turned away and began prying open a canister of cocoa. "That bad, huh?"

"That bad."

Pouring some of the powder into two green mugs on the counter, he went on, "Some father I am. You have to nearly drown yourself to get my attention."

"It worked, didn't it?" She managed a grin. "You used to say the first quality of a historian is resourcefulness."

Thoughtfully, Jim mixed some powdered milk in a pot. "Guess I don't blame you for feeling that way." He sighed. "Too bad you didn't like the old stories, though. Telling them to you gave me a chance to work through my theories about Merlin."

"Well, I did sort of like the ones when he turned King Arthur into different kinds of animals."

"You especially liked the one about Arthur becoming a fish. You made me tell it every night for a month." He lowered the pot of milk onto the still-sputtering burner, then winked at her. "So I'm not a total failure as a storyteller after all?"

She eyed him for a moment. "Almost total."

"Thanks," he replied. "Do you, by any chance, remember any of the stories about the Thirteen Treasures?"

After a long pause, she replied, "The Thirteen Treasures of the Isle of Britain. Merlin had to search for years before he found all of them."

"Almost all of them."

"Whatever. Then he took them to a secret hiding place called the Glass House."

"That's right. Nobody knows where the Glass House might have been, only that Merlin planned to store the Treasures there until the prophesied return of King Arthur. He believed that Arthur would need them to win the Final Battle."

Jim checked his watch. "Hold on. I'll be right back." He stepped to the door, opened it, ducked his head and walked out on the deck. His first stop was the machinery bolted to a metal stand in the middle of the deck; his second, the buoy bobbing just off the stern. The chill, salty air of the sea flooded the cabin, as did the sound of waves sloshing against the boat. And, in the distance, another sound, humming steadily, that made Kate's stomach clench.

In a few seconds, he returned and shut the door. "I'll know pretty soon whether I got any data before the accident. Now . . . where were we?"

"The Thirteen Treasures."

"Right." He gave the milk a stir, then asked, "Can you

remember which was the one Treasure Merlin wanted most? The one he thought was more powerful than all the others combined?"

Kate's brow furrowed, as she listened to the *kerslap, kerslap* of the waves on the hull. "It wasn't . . . the sword of light. Or the cauldron of knowledge. Or the knife that could heal any wound." Her eyes roamed the cabin, coming to rest on the pair of green mugs. "I remember! The thirteenth Treasure. The magical drinking horn."

His gaze seemed to peer right through her. "The Horn of Merlin."

"But what does all this have to do with the ship?"

"Everything." Sliding into his chair, he leaned back and said, "In all the years I've been studying Merlin, no element of the legend has been more fascinating—or frustrating—than the Horn. It's kept me awake for more nights than I can remember. The trail has led me to Cornwall, Normandy, Iceland, Italy, Spain, and now here. And with very little to show for it. Until recently."

He doused his finger in the pot of milk. Shaking his wet finger, he declared, "As it is, I still don't know much. But what I do know is . . . intriguing.

"The story of the Horn has two parts. The first part begins long before Merlin ever found the Horn, in a forgotten land called *the place where the sea begins*. It concerns a legendary craftsman, Emrys, his love for someone named Wintonwy, and the origin of the thirteenth Treasure. The second part is even more mysterious—the part that concerns the whirlpool and a certain Spanish ship."

"The *Resurrección?*"

"None other." He searched her face. "Care to hear a story?"

Kate half smiled. "Better be a good one."

"You can be the judge of that." He reached over and squeezed her forearm under the blankets. "Make yourself comfortable. This will be like old times."

IV

The Story of the Thirteenth Treasure

Long ago, in a land beyond reach and a time beyond memory, a great craftsman lived alone on a mountain precipice. Only the eagles knew where to find him. Yet even they did not visit, for they, like all the creatures of this land, were not welcome.

His true name has been lost from memory, but he is known in legend as Emrys of the Mountain. So vast were his skills that he required no helpers, no messengers. Indeed, Emrys needed no one even to bring him food, for he had devised ways to make stones into loaves of bread, snow into cheese, water into wine.

Such solitude suited his purpose, for Emrys wanted no one else to understand the secrets of his craft. His knowledge was hard won, and he hoarded it greedily. He refused all offers to sell either his skills or his creations, for he held no interest in riches or titles or the ways of men. Any visitors who, by design or chance, came near his alpine hold returned with both empty hands and empty thoughts, able to recall nothing of what they had seen.

Emrys almost never ventured forth, except when he needed to gather the few substances that he could not himself manufacture. He worked ceaselessly, since his work was his only passion. Yet he rarely felt satisfied with the fruits of his labor. He destroyed any creation that he did not deem utterly perfect.

After all his years in the mountains, only twelve creations met his standards, and only twelve did he retain. They were his Treasures. First he forged the sword of light, so powerful that a single sweep of its flashing blade could kill any creature, whether made of flesh or of spirit. Then he made the ever-bubbling cauldron of knowledge, the whetstone that could turn a strand of hair into a gleaming blade, the halter that could make an ordinary horse run like lightning, and the pan that produced the world's loveliest smells. Next came the mantle that could turn its wearer invisible and the ruby ring that could control the will of others. To these Emrys added the inexhaustible vessel of plenty, the harp that could make haunting music at the merest touch, the knife that could heal any wound, and the chessboard whose pieces could come alive on command. Finally, he designed the flaming chariot, whose fire came from the very heart of the Earth.

Yet with all his Treasures, Emrys still lacked one thing. He remained mortal. He was destined to die like all mortal beings. In time, his hands would lose all their skill, his mind would lose all its knowledge. The shadow of this fate so darkened his days that, at last, he could bear it no longer.

In desperation, he left his mountain lair to search for the secret of immortality. He had no idea whether he could find such a thing, but he knew he must try. He brought with him only two of his Treasures: the sword of light and the ruby ring that could make others do his bidding.

His quest led him to many wondrous lands, but he did not stay long in any of them. Emrys searched and searched, following every clue he encountered, but without success. Nowhere could he find the secret that he craved. No one could help him.

At last, after many years of searching, he finally gave up. He made ready to return home in despair.

Then, as he sat in the shadow of a great tree, he heard a young mother telling her child a story. She told of a mysterious realm beneath the sea called Shaa. Only mer people, half human and half fish, lived there. No one but the mer people could find their way to Shaa, though many had tried. All anyone knew was the legend that it lay in *the place where the sea begins, the womb where the waters are born*. Merwas, emperor of the mer people, had ruled the realm of Shaa with wisdom and dignity over many ages. In fact, it was said that Merwas had discovered a way to live far beyond his time, that he could remember the birth of islands that men considered older than old.

To most listeners, this tale would have been nothing more than a simple child's entertainment. Yet to Emrys, it held a seed of hope. He vowed never to rest until he discovered whether the ancient ruler Merwas still lived beneath the waves.

But where was this land of Shaa? *The place where the sea begins, the womb where the waters are born*. It was not much of a clue, but it was all that Emrys had.

With his superior skills, he fashioned a hood that allowed him to breathe underwater with the ease of a fish. He descended into the sea, full of renewed hope. Yet soon he began to realize the enormity of his challenge. The realm of Shaa, if it did exist, would be nearly impossible to find. So vast were the many seas, he would have barely begun his search before his remaining life ran out. Still, he vowed to persist.

Years passed, and although he followed many leads under the sea, he was ever disappointed. Even his ring of power and his flashing sword could not help him. He began to wonder whether he had really heard the story of Shaa at all, or whether it was only a remnant from his fevered dreams.

One day Emrys smelled the sweet aroma of an underwater plant called apple-of-the-sea. It reminded him of apple blossoms in the spring. For a moment he felt captivated by the perfume, and he strolled in memory through apple groves he would never again see on the land.

Then, out of a crevasse before him, a strange form arose. First came the head of a woman, with long black hair flowing over her shoulders. She seemed darkly beautiful, although her eyes were shadowed, almost sunken, so that they gave the impression of being bottomless. With a gasp Emrys realized that, below her shoulders, her body was nothing more than a cloud of dark vapor, curling and twisting like smoke. Two thin, wispy arms formed out of the cloud, one of them clasping a dagger in its vaporous hand.

"Who are you?" asked Emrys, his own hand on the sword of light.

"Nimue issss my name." Her voice hissed like steam vapor.

"What do you want from me?"

She pointed at his ruby ring. "It issss beautiful."

Emrys drew back.

Nimue watched him, coiling and uncoiling her vaporous arms. "It would sssseem a ssssmall pricccce to pay . . . to find the ssssecret entrancccce to the realm of Shaa."

"You know the way to Shaa?"

"An enchantresssss knowssss many thingssss."

Emrys hesitated. The ring had helped him often over the years. Yet he knew also that soon he would die and the ring would then serve him no more. Although it was probably folly to trust the enchantress, what did he have to lose? Giving Nimue the ring seemed a small price to pay for a chance to achieve immortality.

So Emrys agreed to the bargain. Nimue took the ring and scrutinized it carefully with her bottomless eyes. Then, wordlessly, she beckoned to her servants, a band of enormous eels with triangular heads and massive jaws who had been hiding in the shadows. Emrys knew at once that they were sea demons, among the most feared creatures in the ocean. His blood chilled at the very sight of them.

Yet the sea demons did not attack. They merely surrounded Nimue with their slithering bodies. Cautiously, Emrys followed as they led him some distance to the mouth of a deep abyss dropping down from the bottom of the sea. Here, declared Nimue, was the entrance to the secret realm ruled by Merwas.

Then Emrys noticed that the abyss was guarded by a monstrous beast of the sea, a spidery creature with many powerful legs. Though the creature had only two narrow slits for eyes, it seemed to sense the presence of intruders. Its huge jaw opened a crack, revealing a thousand poisonous tongues.

"Treachery!" cried Emrys. "That monster will never let me pass."

But Nimue only laughed and hissed, "I ssssaid I would bring you to the door. I did not ssssay I would open it for you." With that, she turned her vaporous form and melted into the dark waters, followed by the sea demons.

Before Emrys could decide what to do, the monster stirred

and suddenly attacked. Wielding the sword of light, Emrys battled bravely, but the spidery creature pinned him against an outcropping of rock. With a last thrust of the sword, Emrys cut off one of the creature's legs. As it shrieked in pain, Emrys slipped past and escaped into the abyss.

Darkest of the dark, the abyss plunged downward. Emrys, wounded and weak, followed its twists and turns, doubting he would ever reach the end. And even if he did, who could tell whether this was indeed the route to the land of Shaa? More likely, Nimue had tricked him yet again.

Then, at last, the abyss opened into an undersea cavern as wide as a valley. Water so pure it seemed to glow dripped from the high ceiling, gathering into waterfalls that tumbled radiantly into the lake filling the cavern. Fragrant winds, bearing all the smells of the sea, flowed through the cavern's airy spaces. *The place where the sea begins, the womb where the waters are born.* At the far end of the cavern rose a magnificent castle made of streaming, surging water, its turrets and walls as sturdy as glass yet as fluid as the ocean itself.

Instantly, Emrys found himself surrounded by mer people, glistening green. They appeared unafraid and rather amused by his curious form. They escorted him to the shining castle and brought him to the great hall, which was filled up to the base of the windows with water, allowing the mer people to come and go easily. There, seated upon a crystalline throne, was their ruler, a mer man whose eyes flamed brighter than lightning bolts and whose long, white beard wrapped around his waist and prodigious tail. At long last, Emrys stood before Merwas, ruler of the land of Shaa.

When Merwas demanded to know what purpose had brought Emrys there, and how he had discovered the way into Shaa, Emrys told him of his quest to find the secret of immortality. Yet Emrys chose not to reveal that he had been helped by Nimue, fearing that the mention of the enchantress would make Merwas suspicious. The ancient ruler listened carefully, then declared, "Your search, though valiant, has been in vain. I have nothing to give you except a brief rest while you heal your wounds and prepare to return to your home." Then, in a voice like waves crashing upon the cliffs, he added: "You have much yet to learn."

Despite the beauty of this land under the sea, for Emrys it seemed utterly bleak. His quest lay in ruins. He wished he could just lie down and die, rather than attempt the long journey back to his mountain lair.

Then, while wandering alone through the corridors of the castle, he chanced to meet Wintonwy, the only daughter of Merwas. The bards of that realm had long celebrated her virtues. Sang one:

> *Graceful as coral, true as the tides,*
> *Constant as currents the rising moon rides.*
> *Fresh as the foam, deep as the sea,*
> *Bright as the stars, fair Wintonwy.*

For the first time in all his years, Emrys fell in love. He set to work, crafting for Wintonwy a bracelet of gleaming bubbles and other wondrous gifts. Although Wintonwy ignored him, Emrys hoped that his attention might eventually touch her heart.

And, in time, Wintonwy took notice of him. She invited him to join her on a voyage through Shaa. They set off immediately and traveled to the farthest reaches of the realm.

One day, as they camped near a fountain of warm water, Wintonwy chose to explore alone while Emrys designed a new creation. Suddenly, he heard her screams. He leaped to her aid and found she had been attacked by a vicious shark. Seeing he could not reach her in time, he hurled the blazing sword of light with all his strength. It struck the shark in the eye just before the ferocious jaws clamped down on Wintonwy.

She was badly injured, but alive. Emrys carried her in his arms all the way back to the castle, singing continually to ease her pain. Upon seeing them, Merwas raced to join them. Although the old emperor worried how a shark had managed to enter the realm, he chose not to dwell on such concerns, overcome with relief that his dear Wintonwy was safe. In gratitude for saving her life, he asked Emrys to make a wish—any wish.

"To spend the rest of my days at your court," answered Emrys without pause.

"Then you long no more for eternal life?"

"No, my king. I long only to live my life anew at Wintonwy's side."

Bowing his head, the emperor declared: "If my daughter agrees, your wish shall be granted."

Soon the castle came alive with the announcement of their wedding. While Wintonwy prepared for the ceremony, Emrys labored to make a wedding gift of unrivaled elegance. On the eve of their marriage, he unveiled it, a drinking horn whose beauty surpassed anything he had ever made. It was shaped like a spiraling shell, and it glimmered with the light of stars seen through the mist. And, remembering his mountain home, Emrys endowed the drinking horn with a special virtue. Anyone who held it near could smell the fragrant air of the mountaintop, even if he did so at the bottom of the sea. He named it *Serilliant,* meaning *Beginning* in the mer people's tongue.

Emrys offered it to Wintonwy. "I give you this Horn, the most lovely of my Treasures, as a symbol of our love."

"Our love," she replied, "is all we shall ever need to drink."

The Emperor Merwas then came forward. "I have decided to give to Serilliant a special power, the greatest I have to bestow."

"What is this power, my father?" asked Wintonwy.

"It is . . . a kind of eternal life, but not the kind most mortals seek. No, I give to this Horn a power far more precious, far more mysterious."

"Can you tell us more?"

Merwas lifted the Horn high above his head. "I can tell you that the Horn's new power springs from the secret of the newly born sea, the secret we mer people have guarded for so long."

As he spoke, the Horn swiftly filled with a luminous liquid, as colorful as melted rainbows. Then Merwas declared, "Only those whose wisdom and strength of will are beyond question may drink from this Horn. For it holds the power to—"

Merwas never finished his sentence. The castle gates flew open and Nimue, leading an army of sea demons, drove down on the helpless mer people. The sea demons, growling wrathfully, slew anyone who stood before them.

As Nimue aimed her black dagger at Merwas himself, Emrys raised the sword of light in wrath and charged. But just before he could strike her down, Nimue held up one vaporous hand. On it rested the ring that Emrys himself had once worn.

"Look into thissss ring," commanded Nimue. The ring flashed with a deep ruby light.

Emrys froze.

"Now," she continued. "Drop your ssssword."

Unable to resist the power of the ring, Emrys shuddered, then dropped the sword of light.

"Good." The enchantress laughed. "I could kill you, but I will not becausssse you have been quite ussssseful to me. You wounded the sssspider monssssster, allowing me at lasssst to enter the realm of Shaa."

Emrys wanted to pounce on her, but he could not find the strength to move.

"Go," ordered Nimue.

Haltingly, Emrys turned and left the castle.

When at last the invaders departed, both Merwas and his beloved Wintonwy lay dead. The few mer people who survived fled the castle, leaving it abandoned forever. They scattered far and wide, becoming the most elusive creatures in all the sea.

Yet Nimue's triumph was not complete. The Horn somehow disappeared during the battle, and neither she nor her sea demons could discover its whereabouts.

Emrys, stricken with grief, eventually made his way back to his alpine lair. There he resumed the life of a recluse, but never again did he create any works. He did not even try. For the rest of his life he bore the pain of the love he had found and so soon lost. Worse yet, he bore the pain of knowing that but for his own folly, fair Wintonwy would still be alive.

V

THE BALLAD

What a sad story," said Kate, swaying with the rocking of the boat. "But what does it have to do with Merlin? Or the sunken ship?"

Her father poured hot milk into the mugs and handed one to her. "I told you that the story of the Horn has two parts."

"You mean . . . Serilliant . . . became the Horn of Merlin?"

"Yes! Merlin, in his search for the Thirteen Treasures, finally found it, the most precious Treasure of all. He kept it with him for a time—though for some reason he didn't take it to the Glass House with the others. And then, somehow, he lost it."

"Lost it? How?"

"Nobody knows."

Kate's eyes fastened on her father.

"Losing the Horn must have been a terrible blow. So terrible that I'm convinced it finally killed him."

She squeezed some of the water from her braid, then leaned forward. "So what happened to the Horn?"

"I've been trying to answer that question for years."

She watched his face, anxious but determined. "And you think finding the *Resurrección* will help you do that."

"That and more."

Clasping her mug with both hands, she inhaled the rich, chocolate aroma. The memory of the whirlpool's icy waters now seemed far away. "Dad," she asked quietly, "what is this all about?"

He ran a hand through his bristly hair. "I suppose there's no harm in telling you. We're almost out of time. And unless I can get a sonic picture that shows something, this whole project is as sunk as the *Resurrección.*"

"Maybe Isabella can talk the government into an extension."

"I doubt it," he said dispiritedly. "She did phenomenally well to get us a permit in the first place. They have strict rules against people coming down here, you know. Whirlpools and killer shoals don't fit the tourist paradise they're trying to promote. It was only because of Isabella's stature as a scientist that they let us in at all—and then only for a month, with no extensions possible. Still, I was certain that would be enough time to find some hard evidence about the ship. Then, with the prospect of all that gold bullion, they'd be sure to change their tune and grant an extension. But here we are, with just three days left."

Jim set aside his mug and stood up, his frame almost filling the cabin. He stepped to the counter and punched a few commands onto the computer keyboard. With a scowl, he studied the screen. "Nothing yet. We'll give it just a bit longer, and if there's still nothing, we'll fix up the buoy and try again."

"After you tell me what's going on."

Returning to his chair, he said, "All right, you win. But first, you've got to promise me *never* to tell anyone what I'm about to tell you. Not even your mother, not even Isabella. The risks are too great. Do you understand?"

Kate swallowed, but not her cocoa. "Yes."

Jim stared into his mug for a moment before speaking. "For starters, if the Horn of Merlin could be recovered, it would put to rest all the doubts about whether Merlin himself really existed."

"But how?"

"There is only one Horn of Merlin, and its life was so closely intertwined with the wizard's, at least for a time, that from the standpoint of history they have become inseparable. If one existed, so did the other. And if the Horn still exists, it will be simple to recognize—not so much by its spiral shape and rainbow fluid as by its power."

"You really believe it has some sort of magical power?"

"I do."

She scrutinized him. "This is about more than just history, isn't it?"

"Right you are. We're talking about the Horn of Merlin! Many people—and many forces beyond our comprehension—would go to enormous lengths to get it if they knew it still existed."

Kate looked at him skeptically. "You mean like that enchantress Nimue?"

He nodded gravely. "They could have human forms. Or others. I'm talking about forces that thrive on pain, injustice, chaos. It makes me shudder just to think what they might do with the Horn . . . although the true nature of its power remains unclear. Merlin must have known what it was, but he never shared the secret with anyone else."

"Emperor Merwas, in your story, said the Horn's power had something to do with eternal life."

"He said it was *a kind of eternal life, but not the kind most mortals seek.*"

She frowned. "What's that supposed to mean?"

"Don't ask me. But it does give you an idea of the magnitude we're dealing with."

Swallowing some more cocoa, Kate couldn't shake the feeling that her father knew more than he was revealing. Yet she felt reluctant to press him too hard, since he was being so uncharacteristically open with her. Better to try an indirect approach.

"There are lots of legends about the Horn, aren't there?"

"Plenty," he responded. "In the centuries since it disappeared, the Horn of Merlin has popped up in all manner of folklore, all over the world. I'm up to thirty-seven languages, and I've been looking hard for only a few years. But none of the references says anything specific about the Horn's power. It's always *the mysterious Horn, the marvelous Horn, the wondrous Horn,* and the like. And none of the references talks about the Horn actually appearing again. None . . . except one."

"Which one?"

Peering straight at her hazel green eyes, he said, "That reference came from right here. It was an old ballad, known only in the fishing villages in this part of Baja, about the wreck of the *Resurrección*. It was Isabella who first told me about it, more than three years ago. Over coffee in the faculty lounge. She thought it was just another bit of Merlin trivia, having no idea that the reference to the Horn was so unusual. But I checked her translation, and there it was."

Kate took a final slurp of cocoa. "Can you remember how it goes?"

"Can I remember? I haven't been able to get it out of my head now for years." He cleared his throat. "Starts like this:

> *An ancient ship, the pride of Spain,*
> *Embarked upon a quest*
> *To navigate the ocean vast*
> *And still survive the test.*
>
> *It carried treasures rich and rare*
> *Across the crashing waves*
> *Beyond the flooded fields that are*
> *So many sailors' graves.*
>
> *Its goal to link the Orient*
> *With distant Mexico,*
> *The ship set sail with heavy hearts*
> *And heavier cargo.*
>
> *The galleon brimmed with precious gems,*
> *Fine gold and silver wrought,*
> *Silk tapestries and ivories*
> *And spices dearly sought.*
>
> *From China, Burma, Borneo,*
> *Came crates of lofty cost,*
> *And one thing more, the rumors said:*
> *The Horn that Merlin lost.*"

Kate listened, feeling the boat surging on the swells. *"The Horn that Merlin lost."*

"Yes, but note that it says *the rumors said*. Not a very reliable reference! It could mean that the Horn was on board, or that the ship was destined somehow to encounter the Horn, or something else entirely."

"The *Resurrección* has plenty of its own legends, doesn't it?"

"More than its share," he agreed. "You've got to remember, not many sunken ships are surrounded by so much controversy. Some people think that it never existed, or if it did, that it carried nothing of value. But if you ask the villagers around here, they'll swear it went down off the coast, although they can't give you any proof. And a few historians agree, saying that when it set sail from Manila it was carrying enough treasure to wipe out the entire war debt of Imperial Spain. That's more than ninety million dollars in today's currency."

"So why hasn't anybody tried to find it before?"

"I guess no one was crazy enough. First, it's hard to raise money to pay for an expedition when the very existence of the ship is in doubt. Second, the ocean bottom is deep around here, averaging half a mile. Third, there is the matter of the whirlpool. I don't need to elaborate on that."

"No," she said weakly.

"I will say this, though," he continued. "The whirlpool itself has been rather elusive. Since it's almost always covered with mist, and since these waters are so dangerous for sailing, very few people have ever actually seen it. Or have lived to tell about it."

"Let's talk about something else."

He gazed at the steamy window of the cabin. "Come to think of it, the shroud of mist is a little like Avalon. It was the mist more than anything else that made Avalon seem to King Arthur less a real place than an enchanted dream, less part of his own kingdom than the Kingdom of Faërie."

When he spoke again, his voice was barely audible. "Some of the villagers had another name for the whirlpool besides

Remolino de la Muerté. They called it *el lugar donde empieza el viento,* which means *the place where the wind begins."*

Despite her visceral feelings about the whirlpool, Kate found herself slightly intrigued. "That makes me think of the realm of Shaa. You know, *the place where the sea begins."*

"Sounds similar, I admit," said her father, adopting a professorial tone. "But just because two things sound alike doesn't make them related. It's like a billion other coincidences throughout history."

"But you jumped on a coincidence when you heard Isabella's ballad," objected Kate. "You put this whole project together on the basis of one little reference to the Horn."

"Not quite," Jim answered. "The ballad was my first clue, to be sure. But I didn't get really serious about this thing until I discovered something else."

"What else?"

"You might recall I went to Spain a couple of years ago for a conference. Well, I took the opportunity to search through the Spanish archives in Seville, hoping to find something that would help me determine whether the *Resurrección* really existed. Eventually, I did turn up something—although, strangely, it was filed in the wrong place."

"What was it?"

"Some papers that appeared to be the original ship's manifest for an unnamed galleon that sailed from Manila in 1547. When I checked through all the details, it matched to a tee the other surviving descriptions of the *Resurrección.* There was one thing odd about it, though."

A large wave splashed against the hull, jostling them both. Kate leaned closer. "Odd?"

"Yes. Along with all the other items on the list—gold and

silver, jewelry and tapestries, spices and ivory—there was some kind of strange marking. Like nothing I'd ever seen before."

"What did it look like?"

He took his clipboard and drew a design. Tearing off the page, he handed it to her.

"Like this."

Kate puzzled over the mysterious marking. "Somebody's signature?"

"More like a code," her father replied. "Look at that spiral in the middle."

She looked up at his lanky form swaying with the movement of the boat. "A code for what?"

"That's what I wondered, too. I tried to find a way to decipher it, not really expecting I'd succeed. The trail got incredibly complicated, and I got involved with other projects, but something kept me from giving up completely.

"Then one day I was doing some research on a little-known language that is said to have been developed by some of the followers of Merlin in medieval times. They were a strange bunch, many of them doubling as monks, and they had some sort of secret society. Their language is related to Ogham, an ancient Druid alphabet, with some important twists. Suddenly I realized that it looked a lot like the marking on the manifest. So, for the heck of it, I tried to translate it."

She twirled the page in her hands. "And?"

Jim turned the page right side up. "It said . . . *Serilliant.*"

"The Horn? So it really was on the ship?"

Jim stroked his chin. "It could be nothing more than a hoax, a medieval prank of some kind. Yet, if it's true, and if the Horn could be recovered . . ."

As his words trailed off into the sound of splashing waves, Kate felt again there was something else, something about the Horn, that he was not telling. She folded the page and slid it into the pocket of her wet cotton shirt on the floor. Still, what did it matter? He had told her more than anyone else about his dreams. Even if they were destined not to come true, he had shared them. With her.

"Dad, what did Merlin look like? Sometimes I try to picture him in my mind, but it's hard."

"How do you picture him?"

"Tall," she answered. "Even taller than you. With a bent, pointed hat that made him look even taller. Straight, white hair, flying in all directions, like hay. Probably a big wart on his nose."

"That's the archetypal form, all right. But the evidence suggests he looked different than you think."

"No pointed hat?"

"No pointed hat. The only two things he wore constantly were the Horn—for the years he had it—and the blue cape, the one decorated with stars and planets that he used to bring light to dark places."

Kate ran her finger along the rim of her mug, considering the image. "You said losing the Horn killed him in the end. How did he die, anyway?"

"He was entombed in a cave by the sea, somewhere on the British Isle of Bardsey. That's about all we know, that and the date: 547 A.D."

"Hey, that would have been exactly one thousand years before the *Resurrección* set sail."

"So it would," acknowledged the historian. "Another co-incidence, no doubt."

"What happened to him?"

"Most people think he sealed himself in the cave perma-nently because he was so distraught at losing the Horn. Yet that's by no means clear. My own view is that he was sealed in the cave by someone else, someone who wanted him out of the way forever."

"Who?"

"His greatest rival, who tried for years to steal his power, and finally, the Horn."

"Who was he?"

"She."

"You don't mean—"

"Yes. I mean Nimue."

"But . . . couldn't he stop her?"

Jim turned toward the window and the moonlit waters beyond. "Apparently not. Perhaps Merlin was so angry at himself for losing the Horn and jeopardizing Arthur's return that he allowed Nimue to finish him off, as the ultimate pun-ishment. Perhaps he had grown arrogant while he had the Horn and underestimated her strength. Or perhaps . . . she had some help."

"Help?"

"Some sources indicate that Garlon, a legendary seaman of the time who seemed to have had a personal grudge against Merlin—I have no idea why—teamed up with Nimue."

Kate sighed heavily. "She and Merlin must have really hated each other."

"That's an understatement. I imagine, though, that be-neath their bitter rivalry, there was some mutual respect. Maybe, even, a kind of admiration. After all, they did share some things in common, like their fascination for the sea."

"Sounds like that's about all they shared."

"I wish I knew! You have no idea how many conflicting theories there are surrounding Merlin. For example, there's a mountain of good evidence that he died in the cave. Yet there are some people who still maintain that he descended into the sea at the end of his life. They point to an old ballad:

> *He that made the wode and lond*
> *So long before in Engelonde*
> *So too made the steormy sea*
> *And the place where Merlyn be*
> *Searching still in mystery.*"

"*Searching still in mystery,*" repeated Kate. "For the Horn, I guess."

"I guess."

"You said Merlin was fascinated by the sea."

"That's right. He spent a good deal of time there. The name Merlin itself comes from the old Welsh word *Myrrdin,* meaning 'Sea Fortress.' "

A vague recollection stirred in her. "And wasn't the first name of Britain something that meant 'Merlin's Isle'?"

Jim's eyes gleamed. *"Clas Myrrdin."*

Placing her mug on the counter next to a pile of printouts, Kate thought of the others, probably still hard at work back at camp. "How did you get Isabella and Terry to come along on this project? They're not interested in Merlin."

"Not in the least! It's a marriage of convenience, that's all. Our interests don't overlap one bit. Isabella is studying one fish in particular that was supposed to be long extinct, but was found recently in the catch of a local fisherman."

"And Terry?"

"I didn't really know him when I asked him to join us, which was risky. But I knew he is a leader in sonic imaging technology, even if he is only in his twenties. He was the first person to merge sonar, much like whales use to communicate underwater, with the same thermal sensing devices used by satellites. I thought, naively, that getting him meant getting to use his equipment. Was I ever wrong. He's been using it to study the unusual volcanic activity off this coast. And he's—"

"A total jerk." She touched the black cable with her bare foot. "Too bad you can't just get Isabella to take you down in the submersible. Then you wouldn't need to use Terry's stuff to get a picture."

"She guards the submersible with her life! Being the director of the Institute's deep-water research program is not nearly as important to her as being the submersible's chief pilot. And she's reluctant to take it down anywhere near the whirlpool, for fear it might be damaged. So unless I can come up with something very convincing, she won't risk it."

Giving the counter a pat, Jim rose from his chair. "It's time." He punched the commands into the computer once again, then waited.

Nothing.

Lips pinched, he shrugged. "Looks like I struck out." He turned toward the door.

"Look," exclaimed Kate, pointing to the screen. Slowly, a hazy image was beginning to form.

He whirled around. Instantly, he activated the printer. For several agonizing seconds, they waited for the hard copy to emerge. At length, a single sheet of paper edged its way out of the printer.

He snatched it up, his face alight, and studied the hazy image. "It's there!" he announced buoyantly.

Kate took the paper, and her heart sank. "It doesn't look like anything," she lamented. "Just a weird gray blob."

"You could call it that," agreed her father. "Or you could call it an underexposed picture of the area below the whirlpool. Here, look closely. Imagine it with five times the resolution, if I had been able to make a complete image. Can you see those three lines? Could be masts. See? Mizzenmast, mainmast, and foremast, with the mainmast broken. And maybe, just maybe, the hull of a ship, viewed from an angle of about forty-five degrees."

She shook her head.

"And look here," the historian went on. "That patch, could it be . . . sails?" Poring over the picture, he muttered, "No . . . no. They couldn't still be intact after four hundred fifty years! The pressure alone down there would have ripped them to shreds." He focused again on Kate. "Forget the cocoa, we should be drinking champagne! There's something down there, no doubt about it."

"If you say so," she answered uncertainly. "Are you sure it's not just a smudge?"

"I admit it's not clear enough to prove anything. It does fire the imagination, though. Even this quality isn't bad for three thousand feet down! I'll give Terry this much. He knows his stuff." His expression darkened. "But he didn't count on the fact that the buoys' sonic beams seem to attract the local whales. It was probably one of them who wreaked havoc on the buoy."

Kate cleared her throat. "Dad, there's something—"

"I still can't believe it," he interrupted, tossing the page on the counter. "By itself, this picture is worthless. Just a smudge, as you said. But a longer shot is going to show us something. Maybe something amazing. I just need to hook up the transmitter dish, and we'll find out."

As he started for the door, she caught him by the pant leg. "Dad, I've got to tell you something."

"Tell me after I reconnect the dish."

Rising under the shroud of blankets, she stood before him. "The dish isn't there."

He grunted as if he had been punched in the chest. "Not there?"

"That's right," she said tentatively. "I saw it . . . dragged off by a whale."

"What? Are you sure?"

"I'm sure."

"No whale could have done that. Not unless he had hands to untie the net."

He reached for the door handle, when Kate placed her own hand on his.

"The whale didn't untie it," she confessed. "I did."

He stared at her in amazement. "You what?"

"And I broke the dish, too. Trying to rescue the whale! He was all tangled up in the net, and I thought he would die for sure unless I did something."

"Did something!" roared Jim. "Kate, how could you be so stupid?"

He flung open the door and pushed past her. She watched helplessly as he strode to the stern, almost tripping on the mass of cables dangling from the metal stand in the middle of the deck.

He leaned over the railing by the buoy and began fishing for any sign of the nylon net or the lost transmitter dish. The splashes grew louder, as did his cursing.

Kate turned away, unwilling to watch. Angrily, she threw her wet braid over her back. She was certain that her father's cherished project was dead. As dead as their brief moment of closeness. And she was certain that she had killed them both.

VI
PIECE OF EIGHT

Grounded from using the kayak, Kate found her only solace exploring the shoreline along the promontory, especially when low tide unveiled a band of beach, a hundred feet wide, stretching between the black lava rocks and the rim of the sea. On one such foray, she pulled off her sandals and loped along the sand, her feet slapping into puddles and sinking into soft depressions.

Her eye caught a tidal pool, and she kneeled to examine this miniature ocean, frightening an orange crab who skittered away sideways. Shoots of eel grass waved in the water, undulating, sheltering the tiny blue fish who zipped in and out of the comely groves. Snail tracks flowed like ski trails down the sloping stones.

Spying a gnarled barnacle as big as her fist, Kate reached into the pool to grasp it when a small explosion burst in the water. She jerked back her hand as a sting ray lifted off the sandy bottom and floated to the far end of the pool. With a mixture of fear and fascination, she watched it move, flapping in slow motion like an underwater bird.

Then, from beyond the mouth of the lagoon, from behind the bank of fog resting on the water, she heard distant voices wailing. Eerily strange, yet hauntingly familiar, the songs of the whales filled the air for a few seconds, then died away.

Kate thought back to when she and her father had returned to camp in the *Skimmer* two days ago. No sooner had they dropped anchor than Isabella had met them on the beach and informed Jim that, despite all her pleas, the government had rejected her request for an extension. In three short days, she had said, they would have to leave the lagoon.

An explosion of activity, and of tempers, had ensued. After much ranting on both sides, Jim had finally convinced Terry to help him attempt to take one more picture. The young geologist had agreed, although he had expressed serious doubts it would be possible without the missing transmitter dish, and even more serious doubts they would find anything at all below the whirlpool. He had made it clear that he would cooperate only because the group's sole hope of remaining past the deadline would be to produce a recognizable picture of the sunken ship. As they had set to work, Isabella had sequestered herself in her makeshift lab, trying to complete her own experiments.

For the past two days, none of them had stopped working, leaving Kate to explore the beach on her own. She moved on, roaming among the rocks, watching striped lizards scurry through the pickle weed and cardon cactus. Spying some water spurting from a siphon hole in the sand, she dug furiously until she uncovered a plump, white Venus clam. She considered digging up the whole colony and preparing the tasty clams for supper, but she quickly discarded the idea, knowing that no one would pay any attention.

As she continued down the beach, she found herself seeing less of her natural surroundings and more of the discarded debris of civilization that had floated ashore even in this isolated lagoon. The beach seemed to be littered with plastic oil containers, stray bottles, beer cans.

"Looking for a message in a bottle?" asked a voice behind her.

She spun around to face a pale-skinned man, heavy in the shoulders and chest, squinting at her from behind his thick glasses. His sandy hair lay twisted in all directions, apparently uncombed for several days.

"Terry," she said in surprise. "What are you doing here?"

He continued to squint at her. "Decided to take a walk on the beach. Do you mind?"

"No, of course not. It's just that I've never seen you take a walk before."

"That's because this is my first. Thought I'd better take at least one before we leave. Tomorrow's our last day, you know."

She kicked at a crab shell protruding from the sand. "I know. I guess that means you and Dad haven't made much progress."

"Only a little. You have no idea what we're up against, technically speaking." Thrusting his hands deep into the pockets of his flaming orange Bermuda shorts, he added in a cutting tone, "We had a bit of vandalism to the equipment."

Her cheeks grew hot. "Look, I apologized already! Three or four times. Isn't that enough?"

"No," he answered crisply, trying to shield his eyes from the sun. "You can't imagine what I put into developing those devices. Both on the boat and on the buoys. To have you come by and rip it all apart . . . well, it's beyond asinine."

"I was just trying to—"

"Save a whale, I know. How sweet. Maybe that will qualify you for the Vandal of the Year award."

"Get lost."

"Is that what you said to my transmitter dish?"

Kate could only stare at him, feeling pain more than anger, regret more than rage. To her consternation, her eyes grew quite misty.

As Terry watched her, rubbing the two-day stubble on his chin, his expression softened slightly. "Consider it over and done with, all right? At least you waited until the end of the month to do it. The truth is, my work wasn't going anywhere anyway. I really need another six months to analyze the weird volcanism of this region."

"Weird?" she asked, grateful for the change of subject.

He wiped some perspiration from his pallid brow. "Suffice it to say that some rather strange things are happening off this coast. Things that can't be explained by plate tectonics and continental drift."

"You mean like the *Resurrección?*"

Terry guffawed. "I'm talking about *real* things. Things you can see, measure, and record. Like the unexplained surges in temperature I've detected on the ocean floor. Not phantom ships that exist for no one but wishful historians."

Again her cheeks felt hot. "You can't say for sure it's not down there."

"I'll grant you, there might be some old fishing boat down there, or something that looks enough like one to pull the wool over the bureaucrats' eyes. That's why we're working like mad to try for another picture. But a Spanish galleon from five hundred years ago? Complete with masts and sails and a load of treasure? Give me a break."

"How can you be so sure? You haven't been down to check."

"Because I believe in the fundamentals of science, that's why! Not in rumors or legends or whatever."

Squaring her shoulders, Kate shot back, "My Dad's proved plenty of legends are true."

"Sure," he replied. "As true as nursery rhymes."

"If he says the ship exists, then that's enough for me."

"That's why you're not a scientist."

"What's the difference?" she demanded. "You take theories and try to find out if they're true. He takes myths and does the same thing."

"Theories you can prove. Myths you can't. That's the difference." He narrowed his eyes still further. "Tell me the truth. Do *you* honestly believe in this Merlin character?"

"My dad thinks—"

"Not your dad. You."

"Well, I . . ."

"Do you believe it or not?"

"Well, no," she said quietly. "But that doesn't mean he didn't exist."

Terry nodded in satisfaction. "At least you're more of a realist than your father. He seems to think that wizards and treasure ships are all over the place, just waiting to be found."

"That's not fair," objected Kate. "Sure, he gets caught up in his dreams every once in a while. Doesn't everybody?" Stooping, she picked up a fragment of a sand dollar. "Didn't you ever want to find buried treasure when you were a kid? To hold in your hand something kings and queens and pirates fought over . . . like a real piece of eight?"

"Not really."

"Too bad." She threw the sand dollar into the rocks. "You missed a lot."

"A lot of bedtime stories." Without another word he turned and started striding back to camp.

VII

An Ancient Ship, the Pride of Spain

That afternoon, Kate stood outside the main tent watching the wind generator twirling slowly in the hot sun. She kicked a clump of sand, spraying it into the air. Several grains flew into her eye.

I couldn't have wrecked things more for Dad if I'd tried, she lamented, rubbing the sore eye.

The roar of an engine arrested her thoughts. She recognized the battered brown van as it chugged into camp, coughed, then lurched to a stop by Isabella's tent. It was Thursday, and that meant fish market day. The last fish market day.

Isabella, her slight frame made a bit taller by the bun of brown hair piled on her head, emerged from the tent. She looked tired, but not as thoroughly disheveled as Terry. Kate ambled over just as the van's door slid open and an elderly man with sun-baked skin jumped out. In one of his leathery hands, he clasped a net full of fish.

"*Buenos dias,*" he said cheerily to both of them.

"*Buenos dias,*" they answered simultaneously.

That was the last of the ensuing conversation that Kate could understand. Despite her efforts to learn Spanish in school, the real thing went so much faster. She listened to the syncopated rhythms of their speech and the rising inflection at the end of each sentence, trying to catch a word or a phrase.

The old man, moving with surprising agility, spread out the net on the sand. Isabella began examining the fish, peppering him with questions. He answered readily, tugging nervously on his bushy black mustache whenever she paused to inspect the catch.

Finally she pushed aside a larger fish to reveal a rather pathetic, spiny creature with goggle eyes. Catching her breath, she arched her thick eyebrows. Slowly, she said a few words Kate took to mean, "I'll take that one."

Visibly disappointed, the fisherman waved a plumper specimen before Isabella's eyes. But she shook her head and pressed a large clump of pesos into his hand. He quit protesting at once. Then, with the vigor of a much younger man, he packed up the remaining fish, tossed them into the van, and saluted Isabella and Kate.

As the van roared off in a swirl of dust, Isabella studied the fish in her hands. "Amazing," she muttered.

"Pretty ugly," observed Kate.

"No doubt about that, eh?" answered Isabella, still studying the fish.

"You don't expect me to cook it, do you? It wouldn't feed one person, let alone four."

"No," she responded as she pried open the fish's mouth and examined its teeth. "This one is not for cooking."

"What's it for, then?"

"Come see."

As they entered the tent, Isabella brought the fish over to her wash basin and scrubbed it under the rainwater tap. She pulled open each fin and counted the spines before laying it carefully in a pan. Then she dried her hands on her white T-shirt, pulled a fat textbook off the shelf, and began thumbing through the pages.

Kate watched with interest as the marine biologist checked various passages, glancing from time to time at the fish in the pan. At last she turned to a two-page chart showing the evolution of a particular genus of fish. Her slender finger pointed to an illustration of a gaunt-looking fish with oversized eyes. "There," she announced. "Remarkable, eh?"

"That's it, all right," agreed Kate. "Could be the ugliest fish in the book."

"Could be," said Isabella, closing the book. She turned to Kate, her gray eyes dancing with excitement. "More important, though, it's a museum piece. Until recently, everybody, including me, thought this species went extinct several hundred years ago."

Kate looked at the fish with new interest. "So this is the fish you've been studying."

"Hoping to study is more like it. I've been waiting to get my hands on a fresh specimen so I could run a genetic analysis."

"That's what you've been looking for in the submersible?"

"That and other things. As long as I don't go too near the whirlpool, or too close to the bottom because of the recent volcanic activity, there are enough interesting things around here to keep me going for a lifetime."

She reached for her small camera and took several pictures

of the fish, top, bottom, both sides. Then she handed Kate a sterilized mask and put one on herself. Next she donned a pair of rubber gloves.

With a thin scalpel, she slit open the fish, found the spleen, extracted a blood sample and inserted it in a centrifuge. While the machine whirred, she carefully wrapped the fish and packed it into her small propane freezer. A few minutes later, she removed a tiny vial from the centrifuge and carefully transferred the liquid to a petri dish which she placed inside a compact incubator.

Peeling off her mask and gloves, she sat down at her desktop computer and punched in a few lines of information. Then she turned and said, "Fun, isn't it? Like waiting to open a Christmas present."

Kate found the analogy mystifying. "Hard to picture that goggle-eyed thing under a Christmas tree."

Isabella laughed. "The truth is, I feel that way about everything in the sea. That's what comes of growing up in a Mexican fishing village, I suppose. As a child I could hear the sounds of the sea everywhere, all the time, even in my dreams." She waved a hand at her little laboratory. "Seawater covers three fourths of our planet, spawned the very first life, even flows through our veins—yet we know almost nothing about it. Did you know that less than five percent of the ocean floor has ever been mapped, that we know more about the dark side of the moon than we do about the bottom of the sea?"

"No, but I know all I want to know, after meeting that whirlpool."

"Ah, *Remolino de la Muerté*," replied Isabella in her gentle voice. "You are lucky to be alive."

"I suppose so," answered Kate. "Sometimes being alive

doesn't feel so great, though." She tapped the top of the incubator. "Did you always want to study sea animals?"

She laughed again. "Always. That is, after I got over wanting to be a pearl diver. The sea has so many mysteries! Maybe if I live to be three hundred, like some of the folks around here claim to be, I could answer all my questions."

"Do they really say that?"

"Sure, that's what they say. It's a local tradition, eh? Claiming you're older than the sea. No one outside the fishing villages believes it, mind you. But there's no way to prove they're lying, since nobody keeps birth records."

Kate cocked her head toward the tent flap. "How about that guy who brought you the fish? He seems pretty spry for an old man."

"Manuel?" Isabella brushed back a stray strand of hair from her bun. "I don't know how old he is, but that's another curious thing about the villagers here. The old ones, even the ones who say they've lived for centuries, have the energy of youngsters. My mother used to say it's something in the water."

"That would be great if it's true."

Smiling, Isabella recalled, "I used to dream about living to be a thousand." She waited a moment, then asked softly, "And where, I wonder, do your dreams take you?"

Kate started to answer, then caught herself. She walked over to Isabella's little wooden altar by the tent window, bordered by six hand-painted carvings of saints. Beneath the altar sat a long table laden with vials of chemicals, beakers, meters, glass columns, a large microscope, and several more petri dishes. Without facing Isabella, she said, "Someplace where I won't cause any trouble."

"That's not much of a goal."

Kate leaned over the microscope for a few seconds. "It's the best I can do right now."

"Haven't you ever thought about what you'd like to do with your life?"

"I guess so."

Isabella lifted one petri dish to the light and examined it. "And?"

"Well, sometimes when I play softball I think about what it might be like to play shortstop for a real major league team."

"That's a good goal. Any others?"

"No."

"Come, now. Tell me."

Kate thought for a moment. "I suppose sometimes I've thought about . . . about *creating* something, like a book or a symphony or something." Her shoulders drooped. "Right now, though, all I create is trouble. Even when I try to do the right thing, like rescuing that whale, I mess things up royally."

Brushing back some loose hairs from the bun on her head, Isabella said, "I've been meaning to ask you about that, but with everything else going on I haven't had a chance. You're quite sure it was a gray whale?"

"Sure as could be. A young male."

"How was he caught?"

"By the tail, in the net. One of his flukes was almost completely cut off. Blood was everywhere."

"Oooh, that sounds bad. Was he able to swim after you set him free?"

"Hard to tell. He dove out of sight as soon as he could."

"I don't blame him."

Hesitantly, Kate asked, "Do you think he survived?"

Isabella frowned. "No way to know. It's possible. It's also possible that he bled to death, or wound up as food for sharks." Almost as an afterthought, she added, "One thing is certain, though. If you hadn't come along, he would have surely died. You gave him a chance, albeit a small one."

"A lot of good that does for Dad's project."

"You did what you had to do, Kate." She replaced the petri dish on the table. "And who knows? Perhaps what you did had some hidden virtue to it."

"What could be good about destroying the buoy?"

The woman drew in her breath. "For one thing, you made close contact with one of the gray whales who stay here year round. In fact, it may be the first time that's happened since the whalers came here and nearly wiped them out a century ago. The grays who migrate to the Arctic seem to have forgiven, or at least forgotten, those days, but the year-round group has avoided human contact entirely. And since they never seem to stray from the whirlpool, it's been impossible to observe them. All anyone has been able to do is photograph them from a distance and, sometimes, record their mournful songs."

"He did sound awfully sad. But I thought that was because he was dying."

"No, they're always like that. I've never heard anything like it. So sad, beyond what words can explain."

Biting her lip, Kate said, "The worst part is, I really wanted to help Dad on this trip. More than just cooking and doing dishes. I wanted . . . to be his assistant or something. He's always pulling me out of trouble, like he did at the whirlpool. And look what I've done! I've ruined everything."

"That remains to be seen," answered Isabella, examining

the collection of petri dishes. "What feels like an ending might turn into a beginning."

"That sounds nice, but life doesn't really work that way."

Isabella's mind seemed to drift somewhere else for a moment. After a while she said, "Maybe you're right. Our sorrows and our joys do stick with us. Especially our sorrows, it seems." She shook her head, as if trying to banish some unwanted memory.

Then, motioning for Kate to come nearer, she pointed to one of the petri dishes. "There is another side, though. Do you see this little dish? Only yesterday, I put a single cell in it. Now look at it. Multiplied into thousands of new cells already. All from that first microscopic dot."

With a shrug, Kate said, "I don't get it."

Isabella pondered the petri dish for a moment, then tried again. "Something that has always fascinated me about evolutionary biology is that the process never ends. Life keeps growing, changing. Every spiral of DNA is part of the greater spiral of life, a spiral that goes on and on forever. Have you ever thought about that?"

"No."

"Well, to put it another way, you might say *all the future lies within the present*. In other words, the very first single-celled creatures that appeared in the ocean held in themselves all the possibilities of evolution. They were the simplest life you could imagine, more water than organism. I call them *water spirits*. And yet they contained the seeds of fish, dinosaurs, and even humans. Small as they were, they had all the power of creation."

Kate waved at the little wooden altar. "I thought you believed God created everything."

"I do," she replied. "Like a good Catholic. And I believe

in evolution, too. It's just one of God's tools to keep life from getting stagnant. Creation is an ongoing process, as I said. And the best part is, you and I are part of it. You still have in yourself all the possibilities of the water spirit."

Kate stared at her blankly, then moved to the window.

"You're not ready yet to hear this, are you?"

"I'm ready," she responded. "I just don't believe you, that's all."

Isabella moved to the microscope and began sorting through some slides. Finally she came to one that she studied for some time. At length, she exhaled wistfully.

"What is it?" asked Kate, her curiosity aroused.

"Come see."

Kate peered into the lens, adjusted the focus. "Stars!" she exclaimed. "Stars in a night sky."

"Remarkable, isn't it?" grinned the scientist. "They're microbes, found in a single drop of seawater. Yet from this perspective, they look as big as a galaxy."

Raising her head, Kate said quietly, "You know what I like best about looking at the stars?"

"Hmmm. How many stars there are?"

"No. How many *spaces* there are. All those empty spaces between the stars. That's where I can imagine traveling for ever and ever. That's where I can imagine infinity."

Isabella gazed thoughtfully at the microscope. "Just as every star is part of creation, so are all the empty spaces between the stars."

With a nod, Kate turned toward the window flap. She looked beyond the main tent and the wind generator, to the slate blue bay beyond. Numberless rows of gray waves crisscrossed the expanse, broken only by the occasional burst of white where currents collided. "I'll never forget the sight of that whale's tail, all ripped and bloody." She watched the water again. "I read someplace that the whalers used to harpoon baby whales, but not kill them, so their screams would bring their parents close enough to get harpooned. Is that true?"

"I'm afraid so. That's when some gray whales would go wild and try to sink the ships. So whalers called them *devilfish* and the slaughter began. It was a sorry end to a friendship that started out so nicely."

"Nicely?"

"When the first sailors arrived here on the galleons, the whales were still friendly. Not frightened. The crew of the *Resurrección* was even saved, according to legend, by whales who were swimming nearby."

"You're kidding."

"That's the legend. There's the old ballad that I translated for your father. It talks about that, and a few other things just as strange."

Kate moved closer. "Isabella, would you sing it for me? The whole thing?"

She glanced at the timer on the incubator. "I suppose so. We still have a few minutes left, eh?" She waved away some rebellious hairs. "It goes on forever, but lucky for you, I can't remember it all."

An ancient ship, the pride of Spain, she began, her lilting voice describing the ship's fateful journey. Only occasionally did she pause, muttering a few Spanish phrases to herself before continuing. All the while Kate listened, engrossed.

As the tale concluded, Isabella intoned:

> *And so today the ship's at rest,*
> *Removed from ocean gales,*

Surrounded by a circle strange
Of ever-singing whales.

A prophesy clings to the ship
Like barnacles to wood.
Its origins remain unknown,
Its words not understood:

One day the sun will fail to rise,
The dead will die,
    And then
For Merlin's Horn to find its home,
The ship must sail again.

"*Magnifico!*" Kate clapped heartily. "*Magnifico!*"
Isabella bowed in return.

"Can you do that last part again? The part with the prophesy."

She obliged.

One day the sun will fail to rise,
The dead will die,
    And then
For Merlin's Horn to find its home,
The ship must sail again.

"Thanks," said Kate. "Leaves you wondering, doesn't it?"

"A good ballad can do that." Isabella turned to the incubator. "Time to check on our little Christmas present."

"It couldn't look any worse than that fish itself."

On went the sterilized masks and rubber gloves. Carefully removing the petri dish from the incubator, Isabella took a small sample and heated it in a water solution. She then carefully mixed it with a substance labeled *radioactive precursor.* Allowing the mixture to cool, she started draining it through a glass column, injecting new chemicals from time to time.

Seeing Kate's puzzled expression, Isabella explained, "Controlling the ion concentration."

"That helps a lot."

At last, she connected a small meter attached to a photo-electric cell to the glass column. Instantly, the arm of the meter began to quiver, pulsing with a subtle rhythm.

"What does that mean?" asked Kate through her mask.

Isabella did not answer. Seemingly oblivious to everything else, she drew a diagram of a spiraling strand of DNA in her journal, making several notations beside it. Then, meticulously, she cleaned and sterilized her equipment. After that she repeated the entire procedure.

When the meter began bouncing again, recording its invisible quarry, Isabella inspected it closely. Shaking her head, she declared, "This can't be right."

As Kate looked on, the woman cleaned every piece of equipment once more. Methodically, she retraced her steps. For the third time, she connected the meter.

It bounced again.

Isabella grabbed her journal and moved to the computer. There she started entering data until the screen filled with letters, numbers, and symbols Kate could not recognize. Her concentration unshakable, Isabella manipulated the information for some time.

At length, she turned an expressionless face toward Kate. Her voice as calm as the lagoon at dawn, she said simply, "That fish is even more amazing than I thought."

VIII
ONE OUT OF
THREE BILLION

Can't this wait, Isabella?" Jim rubbed his unshaven cheek. "We're almost ready to try another picture. With any luck at all—"

"Luck has nothing to do with it," interrupted Terry, standing in a wilderness of cables sprouting from the back of his computer terminal. He glanced toward the tent flap and pushed his thick glasses higher on his nose. "But we'll never finish if people insist on interrupting us."

Undaunted, Isabella raised the flap to the tent. "If you won't come to the meeting, the meeting comes to you," she declared. She strode inside, followed by Kate, who avoided her father's gaze.

Terry ignored them. "You talk to her, Jim, while I keep working." He continued to tinker with the circuitry.

"Isabella," pleaded Jim, waving a sheaf of printouts in his hand. "Can't you save it for later?"

"No," she replied firmly. "This could be a lot more important than your picture. Believe me, Jim, it's worth your time." She cocked her head at Terry. "And if he wants to miss out on something this big, well, that's his business."

The young geologist looked at her doubtfully. "How big?"

"Big."

"All right," he grumbled, setting down a pair of tweezers holding a microchip. "This better be good."

"Five minutes, no more." Jim stretched his stiff back, dropped the printouts on his desk, and fell into his chair. Leaning back, he propped one foot on the desk, knocking off a barnacle-encrusted shell that had served as a paperweight.

As Isabella started to speak, Kate heard the crash of a wave on the shore and the grinding of sand being sucked down into the lagoon. She would miss this place, its many sounds and smells.

"You know that fish I've been looking for? Well, today I found one, a good adult specimen."

"So?" demanded Terry impatiently.

Isabella paid him no heed. "I did a genetic analysis. Did it three times to make sure there was no error. And I found something truly bizarre."

She sucked in her breath, weighing her words. "The fish has found *a kind of eternal life.*"

Kate glanced at her father, but his eyes were fixed on Isabella.

"What do you mean by that?"

"I mean . . . it would never have died of old age. Sure, it could still be killed, as it was when it was taken out of the water. But that's different."

"Wait a minute," protested Terry. "You said it was an adult. How could it have grown to be an adult without growing old?"

Isabella blew some dangling hairs out of her eyes. "It's rather strange, I admit. The fish looks like an adult . . . except at the genetic level. I can't explain it, but something must have happened to make its genetic structure stop deteriorating. Its DNA shows none of the normal decay that occurs over a lifetime. On top of that, it looks exactly like DNA from fish that lived in this area long ago. It's almost as if the fish . . . became *young* somehow. And stayed that way."

Like the villagers, thought Kate, though she dared not say it aloud.

"That's hard to believe," said Jim.

"It's absurd," declared Terry.

Isabella faced him. "Any more absurd than gene splicing was before somebody did it? Or X rays? Or television?"

"Or continental drift," added Kate.

"Give me a break," snarled the young man. "I don't need geology lessons from you."

"Maybe you need something else, then."

Jim raised his hand. "Quiet, you two." He turned to Isabella. "Let me get this straight. You're saying that this fish of yours is not just a modern-day descendant of some ancient species. You're saying that it's ancient *as an individual.* That it has found some way to live on and on, perhaps forever. Is that right?"

Isabella nodded, as a pair of gulls passed over the tent, screeching loudly. "It's more than that. This fish is not just frozen in time, stretching its life across centuries without decay. It seems to be constantly renewed. Recreated. Reborn."

"But how could that be?" demanded Jim.

"We're all ears," said Terry, fingering a cable.

"Let me give you a theory. It's nothing more than a guess at this stage, mind you, but maybe it will help. Have you ever heard of a disease called progeria?"

No one responded.

"All right, then. Progeria is a rare genetic disorder that

causes premature aging in children. It's horrible to see. Kids grow old so fast that by the time they're nine or ten years old, they look like they're eighty. They develop arthritis, hair loss, bone deterioration, everything. By the time they reach eleven or twelve, they die. And all this happens because one tiny little gene on Chromosome Eight—that's *one gene out of three billion*—happens to be in the wrong position."

Terry checked his watch. "What's this got to do with your fish?"

"Now, it's been proven that some viruses can carry a gene that can change the regulatory system of the host being. So it's possible there is some sort of virus or other substance in the water that can rearrange the genetic material of the sea life around here."

"In the water?" asked Jim.

"Why not?" Isabella replied. "We're only beginning to learn about the strange things that inhabit the sea. You've heard about the undersea volcanic vents—smokers. They breed forms of life that can exist at temperatures above three hundred degrees Fahrenheit, that can live off of sulphur instead of light and air. Like nothing else on Earth."

"So you're saying," pressed Jim, "that something in the water here is altering the genes, causing the aging process to slow down."

"Or even stop."

"But that would mean that creatures could go on living . . . indefinitely."

"That's right," said Isabella calmly. "Think about it logically. Germ cells and cancer cells can reproduce endlessly, making them practically immortal. So might it not be possible, just possible, that the right genetic formula could do the same for us?"

Terry frowned skeptically. "This is ridiculous."

"Is it? In some ways, the fish I examined is not so different from you or me. Our own bodies are constantly replacing themselves, aren't they? Over a seven-year period, every cell in our bodies is replaced. So I suppose you could say that we have some of the same power of renewal. Maybe we just have to learn how to use it better."

Jim considered the notion, like a gourmet savoring a rare delicacy. "You know, legend has it that Merlin somehow learned how to stay the same age. He even figured out how to live backwards, growing younger instead of older with time. The bards called him *oldest at birth, youngest at death.*"

"Hey," piped Kate. "Maybe you should call this thing *the Merlin effect.*"

For the first time in two days, Jim Gordon smiled at his daughter. He then asked Isabella, "Could this—this *Merlin effect* of yours also slow down the deterioration of things that aren't alive, things like wood and cloth and rope?"

"Perhaps, if they're made of organic materials."

"Now look here," said Terry, his normally pallid skin flushed with color. "I've had about enough of this. Are we talking about science—or hocus-pocus?"

Isabella studied him with something like pity in her eyes. "For some of us, the more we learn the less we know."

"Come on, Isabella! You're a scientist. This doesn't stand to reason."

"Reason isn't always enough," she answered. "As a scientist named Einstein once said, *Subtle is the Lord.*"

"Let's get back to the facts," insisted Terry. "Couldn't this fish be just some kind of mutant? A random, isolated case that will never happen again?"

"Sure," answered Isabella. "But it's possible something

more is going on here." She scanned the faces inside the tent, listening to the sloshing and splashing of waves in the lagoon. "Have you ever wondered why this area is so rich in species found nowhere else, or thought to be extinct? Not just fish but crustaceans and porpoises and other things, too. No one, as far as I know, has analyzed their DNA structures, but there is no question now that we should."

Kate stopped twirling her braid. "Are you saying," she asked hesitantly, "that the whales who stay here year round might have been here for ages?"

"Could be. That whale you saved might even have been around when the *Resurrección* went down."

"Sure," said Terry, "and maybe he's also the whale who swallowed Jonah."

Isabella locked into his gaze. "Maybe."

"Nonsense! I suppose the next thing you'll tell us is that Jim's lost ship will rise again, as the legend says."

"Its name is *Resurrección,*" said Isabella softly.

"This is absurd," declared Terry. "Do you really expect us to believe that there is some sort of fountain of youth down there?"

"Not a fountain of youth. Not exactly. More like a fountain of . . . creation. A place that breeds new life in things."

"Enough." He retrieved his tweezers. "I'm going back to work. You people can waste your time if you want to." He dove again into the mass of cables and circuitry attached to the terminal.

Jim, deep in thought, lifted his foot off the desk. "Creation," he muttered, rubbing his beard. "Do you really think that's possible?"

"Theoretically, yes," replied Isabella.

Focusing on a point somewhere beyond the walls of the

tent, he said in a hushed voice, "Imagine . . . a power like that. What it could do. What it could mean."

For a time, they were silent. The tent flap fluttered in the salty breeze, snapping like a flag in a storm.

A moment later Terry tugged on Jim's sleeve. "Give me a hand here, will you? Hold these two cables in place while I check the current."

The historian jolted, then rose from his chair. As Isabella and Kate looked on, Jim and Terry labored to make the final adjustments and connections. They tossed questions and commands back and forth as latches clicked, hinges squealed, keys tapped.

At last, Terry straightened up, walked over to the computer, and announced, "Now or never."

He flicked a switch on a jerry-rigged control panel and pressed *Enter* on the keyboard. The computer hummed steadily but gave no other indication that anything was happening. Then, with a subtle flash, an image started to appear on the screen.

At first a hazy patch coalesced near the bottom of the screen, looking like nothing in particular. A few wavy lines formed above, tilting at steep angles. Numberless dots appeared, then receded, along the left side, as though something was moving in and out of focus.

As the group watched, the image on the screen wavered. It seemed to grow less, rather than more, recognizable.

"What is it?" asked Kate, perplexed.

"Whatever it is, it's useless to us," observed Terry. "Something is malfunctioning."

"And we don't have time to find it and fix it," added Jim in a somber tone. "If only we . . . wait a minute. What's *that?*"

Terry started to adjust the controls, then froze, staring at the screen.

Collectively, they held their breath as the resolution on the screen swiftly deepened. The patch near the bottom took on the dense, curved shape of a great hull. The wavy lines solidified into three masts, two straight, one broken near the base. The dots grouped themselves to the left of the masts, drooping like tattered sails.

"My God."

"It's . . . the *Resurrección*."

Then, inexplicably, the picture began to shimmer, like a reflection in a quiet pool that is disturbed by a stone. All at once, the lines grew fuzzier, the solid places grew lighter.

Terry immediately banged several commands on the keyboard. "What the devil?" he cursed, pounding ever more vigorously.

To no avail. The image of the ship slipped steadily away. Within seconds, it melted to a ghostly shadow, then abruptly disappeared. The screen stared at its viewers, completely blank.

"How could that happen?" demanded Jim. "Is something disconnected?"

Terry shook his head slowly. "Can't be. The terminal is still operating."

"Then what's wrong?"

"Don't know," muttered the geologist, activating the computer printer. "Maybe what we saw was captured in the memory."

After a long pause, a page emerged from the printer. It too was blank.

Terry snatched the page and crumpled it. "I can't believe it," he stewed. "It was almost as if . . ." His words faded away, much as the picture had done.

"Yes?"

"As if . . . something *erased* it."

Jim shook his head. "I don't follow."

Terry eyed him uncertainly. "The only way it could happen is if another set of sonic waves, from another source, canceled out the signals. And there's nothing around here that could do that."

"Oh, yes there is." Isabella stepped forward. "Whales. Gray whales."

"Don't be absurd," said Terry. "Their echolocation isn't nearly as powerful as my equipment."

"What if a group of whales were to project a certain frequency together, in concert? That could do it."

"But that would require a level of intelligence that's never been proven."

"Or disproven."

"You're saying they might be *deliberately* interfering with my sonar?"

"I'm saying it's possible, eh?"

As Terry and Jim traded glances, Kate asked, "Why, though? Why would the whales want to eliminate the picture of the ship?"

"Only they could answer that," Isabella replied.

Jim gazed unhappily at the blank screen. "And we won't be around to ask them. The picture was our last chance."

"We may have one more chance," said a gentle voice.

Everyone turned to Isabella.

"We can try . . . the submersible."

"But I thought you were worried about the whirlpool."

"I am, believe me! We're talking about *Remolino de la Muerté.*" She searched Jim's eyes. "I saw the ship. So did you. We can't leave here without trying."

"How long will it take to get the submersible ready?"

"Several hours," she answered. "We'll need to check everything. Thrusters, fuel tanks, oxygen tanks, pressure housings, the works. And I'll need to insulate the battery pack so the pressure from the whirlpool doesn't cause seawater to short the electrical system. We'll work through the night if we have to."

"I'll be your copilot," volunteered Jim.

"Wait," cautioned Terry. "Are you sure about this? I'd like to stay and complete my work as much as either of you, but I don't want anyone to get killed because of it."

Kate felt a sudden surge of gratitude, a feeling she had not before associated with Terry. "He's right," she declared. "I've seen the whirlpool. You don't want to risk going anywhere near it. Even for the ship. Even for the—"

Her father coughed loudly, cutting her off.

"We'll avoid the vortex—the spinning wall of water—and try to slip underneath." Isabella gathered in her arms a stack of nautical maps. "If the whirlpool doesn't reach all the way down to the bottom, we might be able to hug the sea floor and avoid it entirely."

"Not so fast." Terry pointed at the maps. "The sea floor in this area is spotted with volcanic activity. And my seismograph has been acting strangely. There could be an eruption building. Maybe a major one. I wouldn't want to be anywhere in the area."

Jim pondered his warning. "What would an eruption do to the ship we saw?"

"If it's sitting near the epicenter? Wipe it out, most likely." Terry toyed with the rim of his glasses. "As it would anything nearby. Might even destroy the whirlpool itself, or do some strange things to it."

Jim faced Isabella squarely. "It's your call."

She considered the blank computer screen for a moment. Then she planted her small hand on top of it. "Come. We have much to do before we sail."

IX

THE EYE OF LIGHT

By dawn, they were nearly ready.

As amber light streamed from the east, singeing the peaks of the waves in the lagoon, the ocean breeze blew stronger. Kate stood on the deck of the *Skimmer*. She leaned against the railing, watching Isabella and her father crawl in and out of the silver submersible that floated beside the old trawler. One by one, each item on Isabella's checklist was inspected, tested, adjusted, approved.

Navigation instruments. Depth sounder. Cable winch. Mechanical arm. Hoisting bitt. Batteries.

Watching the process under the steadily lightening sky, Kate knew she could do little to help other than load the odd case or find the occasional replacement part. Terry, meanwhile, had no need for her at all, or at least no faith in her abilities, as he labored to transfer much of his equipment to the metal stand on the *Skimmer*'s deck.

She felt deeply torn about this voyage. She wanted her father's project to succeed. She wanted him to find the ship, to recover the lost Horn of Merlin, to put to rest forever the doubts of those who refused to believe that Merlin truly existed. In a way, his life's work was at stake. Yet . . . so was his life. To imagine him and Isabella willingly flinging themselves into the waters around *Remolino de la Muerté* . . . She frowned, observing the heavy clouds to the south.

Scanning sonar. Camera forward. Camera aft. Viewing ports. Batteries, again.

Kate marveled at how much equipment was crammed into the submersible. Shaped like a bulbous fish, or as Isabella liked to joke, a fat football, it was no bigger than a standard minivan. Yet it held enough gear and supplies to support two people for five days at a maximum depth of seven thousand feet.

Emergency tether. Strobe lights. Floodlights. Titanium sphere. Hatch.

"That's it," pronounced Isabella, pulling herself out of the submersible's hatch and onto the *Skimmer*. She moved to the railing and gently placed her arm around Kate's waist. "Try not to worry," she whispered.

"I'm trying."

At that point, Jim's head lifted out of the hatch. Wedging his shoulders through the narrow opening, he grumbled to Isabella, "Why do you have to drive a subcompact?"

The marine biologist watched him with amusement. "Next you will be knocking my choice of color."

"Silver is fine," he replied, clambering aboard the *Skimmer*. "I'd just like a little more legroom."

Terry joined them. "All set."

Eyeing the conglomeration of hardware Terry had assembled on the deck, Jim said, "You've made my old trawler look more like an oil rig."

The stocky geologist pushed back his glasses. "I'll strike oil before you do."

Isabella regarded him quizzically. "What are you up to?

Those are some of your most specialized instruments, aren't they?"

Terry waved proudly at the metal stand. "I'm trying something completely new. Revolutionary, even. If it works, I'll get a better fix on the volcanic activity on the ocean floor than we have ever had. Than *anyone* has ever had."

"Let's hope it's calm down there today," said Jim.

"Up here, too." Isabella scanned the bank of dark clouds moving in. "I don't like the looks of those clouds."

"Nor do I," agreed Jim. He tugged lightly on Kate's braid. "See you by sunset. Let's have Baja Scramble for supper."

"Be careful," was all she could manage to say.

He turned to Terry. "Turn us loose anywhere near the second buoy. Then hold tight to the steering wheel! I don't have to tell you about the wicked currents out there by the whirlpool."

"No, you don't." Suddenly Terry's face fell. "Damn."

"What?"

"I can't stay at the wheel. After I release the submersible, I've got to operate my instruments."

"But you can't! Someone's got to steer."

"Someone else, then. Maybe you should ride on the boat instead of the submersible."

Jim scowled. "Now wait a minute. This is my opportunity."

"Mine, too."

"You can't do this."

Terry folded his arms.

"Wait a minute, Dad." Kate's own voice surprised her. "I can do it."

"Do what?"

"Steer the boat. I've done it before."

He caught his breath. For a moment he stared at her, swaying to the rhythm of the rocking vessel, then slowly shook his head. "I can't ask you to do that. We'll be out there near the . . . No, Kate, no."

"You didn't ask. I volunteered."

"Sounds like she's willing," said Isabella.

Jim observed his daughter, then touched her nose with his finger. "I'm tempted to say thanks."

"Hold it," said Terry. "What if the water gets rough? I've got my best instruments on board. Are you sure she can handle it?"

Kate's torso stiffened. "I can handle it."

"I believe you," declared Jim. "Let's get going. You take the wheel when Terry goes to release the cable. Got it?"

She nodded.

"And if the waves get heavy, turn into them. That way you won't capsize."

She nodded again.

"And don't forget to put on your life jacket."

"All right," growled Terry. He faced Kate. "Just keep away from my instruments."

"Let's go." Isabella raised her voice above a gust of wind. "The weather's looking meaner."

She scampered over the side and down the hatch of the submersible. Jim followed, more awkwardly. An instant later, his hand reached up and pulled the hatch closed with a *clank*.

Without a word to Kate, Terry raised the anchor, checked the cable connecting the two crafts, and stepped into the cabin. As he turned on the engine, she cast her eyes toward the rising waves beyond the breakers and the heavy bank of mist beyond. She remembered her life jacket, then realized it was in the cabin with Terry. She grasped the railing securely, even as the first drops of rain struck her face.

Slowly, the trawler and its gleaming silver cargo slid into the lagoon. On a good day, with a favorable wind, the *Skimmer* could cruise at seven or eight knots. With a heavy load like this, Kate knew, it would be lucky to make half that speed, although that was still faster than the submersible could move under its own power. As she listened to the straining, sputtering engine, she wondered how long it would take before that noise would be joined by the ominous humming she had heard once before.

The water grew increasingly rough as they reached the mangroves. Submerged in high tide, the trees seemed now less a forest than a green labyrinth concealing many dark mysteries. A massive wave slapped the boat, jostling Kate. She staggered to one side, wrapping her hands more tightly around the railing.

Regaining her balance, she saw the last dune come into view. Soon would come the breakers. And beyond . . . She did not want to think about it. But she could not help herself. Her body tensed, just as another wave flooded the deck, spraying water into the air, soaking her jeans and cotton shirt.

She tried to distract herself by focusing on the submersible, bobbing along behind. How bad was the ride for its passengers? They couldn't be comfortable in there. What would it be like for them to travel below the surface, way below, where light never shines? Someday, perhaps, she would find out. In another ocean, another time.

The boat shook violently as they entered the breakers, twisting her stomach into knots. Feeling nauseous, she looked toward the lagoon. Shreds of swirling fog had started to consume everything, making the camp less and less visible. The rain pelted harder. Before long she could see only the top of the flagpole above the mist, then nothing.

As the *Skimmer* chugged past the first buoy, a brown pelican dropped out of the darkened sky. The bird plunged into the frothy waves, surfacing an instant later with a struggling, squirming fish.

Farther from shore, nearer to death. The words echoed in her head to the cadence of the wheezing engine. *Farther from shore . . .*

Waves of water, waves of fear. The boat pitched wildly from side to side. Wind roared. Lightning exploded in the air, followed by the rumble of thunder, booming between sea and sky, melding with the humming sound that drifted over the sea.

Terry threw open the cabin door. "It's time!" he shouted above the storm.

Kate stepped toward him but slipped on the deck, careening some distance before she could catch herself on the railing. She righted herself awkwardly, then stumbled to the doorway.

"Get the wheel," he commanded. Without closing the door, he hurled himself onto the deck.

Grabbing the steering wheel, Kate twisted the boat into an immense wave just as it swallowed the bow. Glancing over her shoulder, she could see Terry crawling the last few feet to the lever mounted at the stern where the cable attached. Once he released it, Isabella could retract the cable and descend.

Bracing herself, she held tight to the wheel despite the violent swaying. Wave after wave crashed against the hull. Yet she remained firmly planted, holding the boat on course.

It's been more than two minutes, she realized with a start.

Swinging her head toward the stern, she could see Terry struggling to move the lever. He was straining, throwing all his weight into the task. A wave washed over him. He strained still harder. Yet the lever did not budge.

He started to pound at it with the heel of his hand. Then, seeing Kate through the doorway, he called to her.

"The hammer! Bring me the hammer!"

She began letting loose of the helm, when she realized that to do so was to risk a disaster. Grasping the wheel firmly with one hand, she shoved the cabin chair underneath as a brace, scraping her knuckles in the process. She stepped back. It would hold, but not for long.

Pulling her father's old hammer from the box of tools in the corner, she worked her way across the deck, fighting to stay on her feet. At last she reached the stern and handed Terry the hammer. He smashed the lever several times, to no avail.

Just then a great wave collided with the port side. The metal stand bearing Terry's instruments slid perilously close to the railing. He leaped to it, hauled it back, then staggered over to Kate.

Mist wrapped around them, so tightly that they could no longer even see the submersible at the other end of the cable. The swells heaved, the *Skimmer* tossed.

Terry raised the hammer to swat again at the jammed lever.

Then a strange thing happened. The cable to the submersible suddenly went slack—from the submersible side. Kate and Terry stared at each other, thunderstruck, knowing there was no way to release the cable from that end.

Kate leaned over the railing, peering into the impenetrable fog. At that instant, a huge wave hit the hull. The boat lurched sharply. She pitched over the side, though one hand somehow held on to the railing. She hung there, dangling above the raging sea.

"Hellllp!" she wailed. Water sucked at her legs, hauling her downward.

Terry reached his hand toward her, stretching to grab hold. Suddenly he caught sight of his instruments tottering near the edge of the deck. He hesitated for a fraction of a second.

Another wave arched and toppled over the stern. Kate's grip tore loose, and she tumbled into the sea.

She groped madly for the surface, gasping for air. The pounding in her head merged with a clamorous humming sound that swelled steadily.

Panicked, she tried desperately to swim away from the sound. Away from the whirlpool! More waves tumbled over her, sapping her energy. Her limbs weighed like anchors. The *Skimmer* had vanished in the fog and spray.

Without warning, the water grew calmer. An enormous wave seemed to carry her upward, higher than the ragged surface of the sea. Instead of pounding her, the water swirled past, racing around and around in a great circle. Then, to her horror, she saw that below her a dark, yawning chasm was opening: a huge hole in the middle of the ocean.

The hole drew her nearer. She fought to get away, but the dark center expanded, reaching toward her, pulling her down.

The world started spinning. The gray sky above shrank into a vanishing eye of light, shimmering with the moving mist. Everything whirled faster and faster. A wall of blue rose above her, high as she could see.

Then, all at once, the sky disappeared.

PART TWO:
BEYOND THE WHIRLPOOL

X

MIST

A twisted train of dreams besieged Kate as she floated in and out of consciousness. Swirling, undulating images swam into view and then burst apart, scattering into grains of sand. Falling! She was falling downward, ever downward . . . Curling, crashing waves. *Help! I need to breathe!* Falling, spinning, falling, spinning. A family of gray whales, all pouring blood from their severed tails. Someone else, someone she knew. *Dad! Dad, I'm here!* But he could not hear, hidden behind the steel walls of the submersible. Then another figure. Terry. *Reach! Just reach for me!* Still falling . . . Wispy sails. A sunken ship. Waves, more waves, surging and subsiding, pounding her, twisting her back to the point of breaking. Sudden calm. Dead quiet. Sand on her tongue.

Drenched and bruised, she opened her eyes.

She spat out some sand. With effort, she tried to make herself stand. But the dreadful dizziness returned and she fell back, her head whirling.

For some time she merely lay there, her face in the wet sand, waves gently lapping at her sneakers. When at last the spinning slowed enough, she resolved to try again. More slowly this time. She slid one arm forward and planted her hand on the sodden ground. Despite the throbbing in her neck, she rolled to her side.

Fog. Fog everywhere.

She rested, gathering her strength, before daring to try to lift her head again. With a groan, she pushed herself to her knees. The dizziness flowed into her brain like water into a broken boat, yet she held her body rigid, unwilling to relinquish her gains. Then the sand started to sway and slide beneath her and she toppled once more.

She turned slowly onto her back. The world continued to swirl, and the ceaseless spinning seemed to exist as much within her mind as without. Again, she perceived the heavy mist surrounding her. And a salty taste on her lips. Or was that, too, just a dream? Fog curled and billowed, wrapping around her, covering the surface of this little island where she now lay. If indeed it was an island.

Gazing upward at the shifting clouds, she became conscious of a sound. Humming like an army of engines, it seemed omnipresent, coming from everywhere and yet nowhere in particular. It reminded her of the whirlpool's dreadful droning, while at the same time it was somehow different. Then the clouds grew thicker, racing around with increasing speed. Everything she could see began to rotate, whirling endlessly, as if she were stranded in the middle of a cyclone.

Dizzy again, she grasped the ground with both hands, squeezing the sand in her fists. Sheets of mist flowed past, shielding her from the twisting clouds above. All the while the humming sound persisted, vibrating in her ears.

Concentrating on every movement, no matter how small,

she rolled to one side and clambered to a kneeling position. *As long as I don't move too fast, maybe . . .* She rested awhile, then gradually, painfully, lifted herself to her feet.

She took a wobbly step, surveyed her surroundings. The rolling fog obscured all beyond a few yards. This island seemed to be nothing but a low, sandy mound, without much color and without a single tree, bush, or blade of grass. The only vegetation she could see was a purplish algae that rimmed the shore, glistening in the watery light.

Something shiny, half buried in the sand, caught her eye. She stooped to retrieve it, when suddenly the entire island shook with a violent tremor. The ground buckled savagely, knocking her off her feet.

Then, as abruptly as it had struck, the tremor ceased. Kate lay there, tears welling in her eyes. *Am I that weak?* Or did the ground really shake? She tugged lightly on her braid, the way her father so often did.

A deep desire rose within her, a desire to find him, to be with him again. Someplace where the ground didn't shake, or seem to shake. Someplace out of danger.

Out of danger. Those final moments on board the *Skimmer* were so compressed, so cloudy. She could only remember the storm, and Terry starting to reach for her—then letting her fall. Yet there was something else, something about her father, that nagged at the edges of her memory. She knew it was important. But what could it be? All she could recall was the vague feeling that something had gone awry. That he was in trouble.

She shook her head, pushing aside such worries. In not very long he and Isabella would surface in the submersible and make their way back to camp, with or without any help from Terry, with or without some evidence of the sunken ship. *At least the weather is calmer*, she told herself. *The fog may be thick, but that storm seems to be over.*

Haltingly, she forced herself to rise. Dizziness swept through her again, and she placed both palms on the sand for support. Her right hand brushed against a hard object. Seeing the shiny glint again, she closed her fingers around it and pulled.

For an instant the sand held firmly, as though unwilling to part with its prize. Then, with a slurping noise, the object came free, leaving behind a little tomb that filled swiftly with water. She wiped off the wet sand, then held the object before her.

She blinked in surprise. It was a finely wrought comb, carved from white ivory. Upon its back, embellished in gold, shone the face of a woman. With the hint of a smile and sad, loving eyes, she looked almost sublime. *The Virgin Mary? Isabella might know.*

Mystified but exhilarated, she twirled the comb in the luminous mist. Then she slipped it into one of the pockets of her wet jeans. Though her back ached and her knees trembled, she rose once again and cautiously stepped forward. Her feet sank into the soft sand.

But for the undulating mist, nothing stirred. This island seemed totally uninhabited. Not even a solitary crab scurried over the ground. She felt utterly alone.

Cupping her hands, she called into the mist. "Hello! Can anybody hear me?"

No response. She tried again with the same result. It might be ages before anyone found her in fog like this. She could barely see beyond the water's edge. She kicked a clump of sand, wishing it were the face of a certain young geologist.

She rolled up the sleeves of her blue cotton shirt. The

humid mist felt warm, like the inside of a kiln. *Strange it's so hot on such a cloudy day.* She trudged into the fog, leaving a string of gray footprints behind.

A new sound knifed the air. Kate halted, listening. Beyond the continuous humming, a distant scream wavered. Slowly it deepened into a mournful wailing, a wailing she had heard before. Louder it swelled, until joined by other voices, creaking and whistling like winds of pain. Soon it seemed that the sea had found a voice of its own, raised in unending sorrow.

Whales. They were out there, somewhere beyond the fog. *So sad, beyond what words can explain.* That was how Isabella had described their songs.

Then, as she walked, the mist before her shifted, darkened. At first she thought it was nothing more than the same swirling vapors, restless as ever, playing tricks with her vision. But as she watched, the fog seemed to pull apart, to separate, unveiling a hulking form just ahead on the beach.

She stepped backward. The shape grew more distinct, gathering in fullness as the clouds dissipated. She caught her breath, staring in disbelief.

XI

Aт Anchor

Mist swirled around the hull of the old wooden ship, draping the ragged sails like layers of translucent silk. It rested, tilted to one side, in the sand. The mizzenmast leaned precariously toward the bow, pointing directly at Kate. The mainmast still towered above her head, though it ended abruptly in a tangle of rigging.

Cautiously, she moved closer, examining the red-painted hull carefully. One section near the rudder had been smashed apart, exposing a dark cavern at the base of the hull where barrels and crates of many sizes and shapes rested, together with heaps of ballast stones. Dozens of round clay jars hung overhead, lashed to the rigging. Cannons, tapered in the muzzle, protruded from notches. Numerous rope ladders ascended to the sails, covering even the captain's quarters above the stern, giving the impression that the whole ship lay covered with cobwebs.

Approaching the hull, she spied an enormous anchor, planted on the beach. Cast in the shape of a pointed fishhook with double barbs, it looked massive, unmovable. Kate bent to touch the heavy black chain, twisted into knots and curls. She tried to lift one of the links from the sand. It was impossible.

Straightening herself, she surveyed the wreck. It looked eerily like the phantom ship on the computer screen. Yet she knew that was the one thing it could not possibly be. So how did it get here? And when? Her heart told her one thing, her head another.

Her gaze fell to the shaft of the anchor. Some sort of symbol marked it, raised from the iron in bold relief. She threw aside the broken plank that partially covered the spot. There, before her, was a rough circle and within it, *the letter R.*

She glanced upward into the churning mist, lit so eerily from above. *No way. It can't be.*

Using her sleeve, she wiped the salty dew from her face. Hesitantly, she approached the gaping hole in the hull, stepping over ballast stones, splintered timbers, and shards of pottery. She spied a capstan, the rotating wooden drum sailors used to raise anchor before the invention of the mechanical winch, lying on its side on the sand. Next to it sat the top half of a huge earthenware vessel, the kind used centuries ago to store water for long ocean voyages.

Only a few shafts of light entered the hold, leaving most of it in shadows. She paused at the opening, letting her eyes adjust. An odd smell, spicy and potent, wafted from somewhere nearby.

She kicked aside a small bundle at her feet, which clanged against the floor. Curious, she peeled back the dusty cloth to find that it covered an ornamented pitcher. As she held it up to a shaft of light, it shone brightly, and she realized it was made of solid gold, intricately carved with images of a shepherd tending his flock. A fearsome face was carved into the spout. Once in a museum she had seen a gold ewer like this, raised from a wreck in the Caribbean, never dreaming she might hold one in her hands one day. Carefully, she placed it on a wooden crate and moved deeper into the hold.

Boxes, bundles and chests crammed the odd-cornered room. The air smelled damp, musty, with a hint of the strange spicy aroma. Wedged together along the walls, hung from the ceiling, piled on the floor, they seemed too numerous to count. Spying one chest that had been split apart, she drew nearer. From it she pulled a delicate silk cloth of azure blue embroidered with threads of silver that glittered like Himalayan rivers.

Stepping over a pile of ballast, she noticed a group of rectangular stones visible through a hole in the floorboards. She stooped to look more closely. The stones gleamed only dully, but there could be no mistake. Gold. Gold ingots. Dozens, perhaps hundreds, of them. Right under her feet.

Then something flashed by her sneaker. Kate knew what it was before she touched it, before her hand curled around its rough-hewn edge. Lifting it to the light, the silver object glistened. *A piece of eight.*

She hefted the old coin, surprised at how heavy it felt. On one side she saw a Hapsburg shield, displaying the mint mark next to the denomination, a Roman numeral VIII. On the other side, a bold cross. Within its quarters, she could make out two standing lions and two castles. Much of the inscription was illegible, but the words *Carlos I, Rex* were plain to see. As was the date: 1547.

She squeezed the coin in her hand, as hard as she could, feeling it gouge into her fingers. This had to be a dream. Had to be.

Carefully, she placed the coin in one of her pockets. She spied a thin wooden ladder tied to a trunklike column that appeared to be the bottom of the mainmast. Her heart racing, she ascended the ladder, rung by rung, passing through two more decks as full of shadows and cargo as the hold.

Her head bumped into a trapdoor. Heavy though it was, she managed to raise it by pushing with her shoulder. The door fell open with a clunk. She climbed through the hold to find herself standing on the main deck of the ship. Cannons, six to each side, lined the wall. Beside one rested a case of black iron balls.

Kate drew nearer and, with effort, lifted one of the cannonballs. She remembered reading, in one of her father's reference books about galleons, a vivid account of warfare at sea. She imagined sailors heating cannonballs to red hot before firing them at enemy ships, hoping to set fire to wooden decks or blow up powder magazines. Then she spotted another case, this one containing bar shot for ripping sails and rigging. Next to it lay a rammer, a wad hook, a powder ladle, and other tools of cannonry. All this equipment lay idle, useless against whatever force had grounded the ship.

The spicy smell, much stronger than before, tickled her nose. It seemed to emanate from the captain's quarters. Cautiously, she approached. Before lifting the door's polished brass latch, she glanced skyward, through the web of rigging, luminous in the mist.

The door swung open. She had to stoop to pass through it, entering a room much less cluttered than the hold. Much lighter as well, thanks to a glassless window at the stern. The air practically vibrated with the spicy aroma. An elaborate tapestry, depicting a Chinese harbor, hung from one wall. A thin bed, blankets rolled in a mound, lay beside a polished desk made from exotic woods. On the desk sat a quill pen, a jar of black ink, a bronze astrolabe and a sextant for navigation, a double-handled gold cup etched with rows of snakes biting their tails, a candle holder wrought of gleaming jade, and one slender volume bound in red leather.

She touched the book's flaking leather cover. It was old, very old. As old as the piece of eight. As old as the ship named . . .

Shaking her head, she moved further into the chamber. The floorboards, dotted with small stones the size of date pits, creaked underfoot. She ran her finger along the desk's smooth rim. *The captain's quarters.* Noticing a roll of papers leaning against the desk, she unfurled it, finding a collection of intricate maps. She studied them one by one, turning each of them sideways and upside down. Yet she could not recognize any of the images or decipher any of the script.

Baffled, she tossed the roll onto a bulky pile of brown rags stuffed in the corner. The spicy smell struck her again, and she turned to a black cooking pot resting on an upturned barrel by the rags. Leaning over the pot, she saw it contained a thick brown liquid. She sniffed. Cinnamon. Ginger. Clove. And something else, subtle and mysterious.

Just then, she felt an odd sensation. As if something, somewhere were watching her. She straightened up, scanned the chamber. Nothing stirred. But for the omnipresent mist circling outside the window, she discerned no motion, no life at all.

Yet . . . she could not shake that feeling.

She took a deep breath, but her heart continued to beat rapidly. Turning back to the desk, she decided to examine the ancient volume. Maybe it held some clue to all this. She reached to touch it.

Something rustled behind her. She whirled around, then froze.

The pile of rags was moving.

XII

GEOFFREY OF BARDSEY

Slowly, a wrinkled hand emerged from the rags. Another hand followed, then a grizzly gray beard, a hawklike nose, and two coal black eyes beneath wild, scraggly brows.

Both hands lifted high into the air, as the dark eyes regarded Kate solemnly, without emotion. At that instant the beard parted, revealing a wide mouth holding very few teeth, while those it held hung blackened and askew.

Kate started to back away, fearing the old man beneath the rags was preparing to pounce on her. Then he released a bizarre, bellowing noise, one that sounded something like an antique car horn.

He's yawning, she realized in amazement. Anxiety swiftly gave way to curiosity. She watched the man stretch his arms, scratch his bedraggled hair, and pull vigorously on his beard, all the while continuing to yawn.

At length, he ceased. "Drat this infernal heat," he muttered in a rolling, hefty accent. "Makes a man sleepy. A nap's a luxury, I say, but not necessarily for the living." He struggled to stand while reaching for a delicate porcelain dish piled high with some sort of shriveled fruit.

Suddenly he jolted, almost dropping the dish. "My goodness! A guest." Recovering his composure, he extended the dish to Kate. Almost casually, he asked, "Care for a date?"

"Uhh, no thanks," she replied uncertainly.

The old man popped a date in his mouth. "Delicious," he pronounced, spitting the pit onto the floor. "Fresh as could be." A sudden anguish filled his face. "Have we been introduced? I've quite forgotten."

Tentatively, Kate extended her hand. "I'm . . . I'm Kate. Kate Gordon."

The hawklike nose twitched. "Gordon. A Scotswoman, eh?"

"Well, my grandfather came—"

"Delighted," he continued, scratching savagely behind one ear. "Cursed sea lice! Now, where were we? Ah, yes. You were saying where in Scotland you hail from."

"Oh, not me. No."

"A new province, I take it. *O'Naughtmeno*. Fine alliteration. Declared your independence already, have you?"

"No, no. I mean—"

"To learn who I am, I know." The old man scratched again, shaking his unruly hair. Then, to Kate's surprise, he crumpled into a kneeling position, took her hand, and gave it an awkward kiss. "Geoffrey of Bardsey, at your service."

Before she could reply, he let out a piteous groan. *"Ehhh!* Now I've done it."

"Done what?"

"The knee. Old riding mishap. From before I gave up horses—and most everything else, mind you—to become a monk. Would you mind terribly . . . *ehhh,* helping me, *ehhh,* up?"

Kate grabbed him by the arm and hoisted. The old man

struggled to stand, nearly toppling them both. He pulled anxiously on his beard, then staggered to the chair by the desk and collapsed, breathing heavily.

"Are you all right?"

"Right? Oh, yes. Couldn't be better. Nothing a good nap can't fix." His eyes narrowed, and he seemed confused. "Could have sworn . . . Wasn't I just taking a nap?" He scratched, this time the other ear. "Yes, now I remember. A good nap in the corner. Then someone came in."

"Me," offered Kate.

"You?" He fought to lift himself from the chair. "Have we been properly introduced?"

"Yes," she answered, half amused and half exasperated. She eased him back in the chair. "I'm Kate. You're Geoffrey of something."

"Bardsey. So we have."

"Bardsey," she repeated. "Wasn't that the name of the island where Merlin died?"

Geoffrey nodded. "Entombed. By Nimue." His eyes grew moist. "A miserable way to go, that." He stretched his arm toward the porcelain dish, took another date. Chewing it slowly, he turned toward the window, then back to Kate, as if she had reminded him of something deep in his past. At length, he asked, "You know of Merlin?"

"A few of the stories. My dad knows a lot more." She leaned against the desk, her expression grave. "Where are we, anyway?"

The wild eyebrows lifted. "You don't know?"

"How could I know?" she retorted. "It's all such a blur."

"I take your meaning," Geoffrey replied dispiritedly. "And it grows worse with each passing century."

Kate stiffened. "Century?"

The old man's eyes fixed on hers. "You are my first guest in . . ." He paused, trying to count on his fingers, then gave up in frustration. "In many years. Not many people care to pay a visit to the *Resurrección.*"

The name rang in Kate's ears. "That can't be true!"

Geoffrey spat out a pit, wiping his mouth with his ragged sleeve. "Forgive my manners. I've forgotten most of the little I knew."

She seized his sleeve. "But the *Resurrección* got swallowed by the whirlpool ages ago!"

The brown rags stirred uncomfortably. "Ah, yes. A dreadful experience, let me assure you. One I don't plan to live through again." He swept his eyes over the chamber. "Not that I object to these quarters, mind you. Far better than Wytham Abbey, I should say! And well stocked. I could last another half millennium with a bit of rationing. All the best spices, including cardamom from India, to make my tea and freshen the air. Fine tapestries to look at, sea biscuits and garlic to eat, sweetmeats and honey for dessert whenever I please. Not to mention the fresh fish that wash up on shore. And let us not forget the dates! I do love them. The ship's wine I finished off about a century ago, I'm afraid, but I still get plenty of clean water from this vaporous air. I could hardly want more, but for an occasional idle conversation like this."

"This isn't idle," protested Kate. "This is serious! And I still don't believe you. If you went down with the ship, how come you're still alive?"

Geoffrey's mouth gaped wide with another yawn. When finally he finished, he replied, "Oh, I do my best to keep occupied. It does get a bit tedious at times, of course. I keep reminding myself that the word *monk* comes from the Greek *monos,* for *alone.* So perhaps it is my fate to be here. Still, there's not much to do except eat and sleep, pray and count combs."

"Combs?"

The haggard head nodded. "It was the twenty-sixth of May—I remember it so clearly—when the *Resurrección* set sail from Manila, bound for Mexico. We were heavy with cargo, including a big shipment of ivory combs. Lovely ones, carved with Our Lady's image. Thirty-one thousand, eight hundred and forty-three, to be precise." He frowned. "Though for some reason I've been able to find only thirty-one thousand, eight hundred and forty-two."

Feeling the bulge in one of her pockets, Kate's stomach clenched. "So we really are . . . at the bottom of the whirl-pool?"

"The very bottom."

"And the light and air down here—"

"Is carried down the funnel, of course. It's often a bit dusky, I admit, but the light is quite sufficient, unless perhaps you are practicing calligraphy."

Kate swallowed. "You're pulling my leg."

Geoffrey looked puzzled. "Pulling your leg? How could I? I'm nowhere near your leg."

"I mean you're fooling me."

"Not at all," he replied. "If you were to step a mere forty paces from this ship in any direction—not that I would advise it, mind you—you would meet the spinning wall of the whirl-pool. And beyond that, the sea."

"Half a mile down," added Kate. "It's a lot to swallow."

"Yes," laughed Geoffrey. "Even a large whale would have difficulty swallowing so much."

"I didn't mean . . . oh, forget it."

"Don't worry, though. After eighty or ninety more years you will come to accept living inside a maelstrom as a fact of life, as I have. Even your memories of blue sky will fade." He glanced up wistfully. "I should have liked to see it once more, though. Just once."

"But it's not a fact of life!" objected Kate. "I want to see my dad again! And my mom. And Isabella. I'm not going to just sit around here eating dates forever!" Then a new realization dawned. "Didn't you feel that tremor a while ago? There could be an eruption down here. Maybe a big one! It could wipe out the ship, the whirlpool, everything."

Geoffrey yawned once more, this time for nearly a minute. "Quite so," he said drowsily. "I feel another nap coming on."

"No," she insisted. "Not now."

The old man's eyelids closed. "Curious things, eruptions," he murmured. "Most unpredictable."

"Wait!" She shook him by the shoulders. "You can't sleep now. Listen. I think my father's down here someplace. In the submersible. Maybe, if we can find some way to contact him, he could help us get out of here."

Geoffrey's eyes opened a crack, regarding her suspiciously. "What would your father be doing down here?"

Kate started to speak, then hesitated. "He's, ah, looking for the ship."

"He wants the gold and silver aboard?"

"Well . . . not exactly."

"Something else, then?"

She said nothing, remembering her promise not to reveal anything about the Horn. Yet . . . what harm could it possibly do to tell this old monk? It might even elicit his help. On an impulse, she pulled from her shirt pocket a soggy piece of paper bearing a strange design. She unfolded it carefully, then held it before his face. "If you know what this means, then maybe I can trust you."

Geoffrey studied the design, exhaling slowly. *"Benedicite,"* he said in a quiet voice. "So you know about Serilliant."

XIII

THE ORDER OF THE HORN

I know a little," answered Kate.

"Are you," Geoffrey asked, his eyes suddenly alight, "one of *the Order?*"

"The what?"

"The Order of the Horn." Geoffrey pushed himself out of the chair. He clasped Kate in an enthusiastic embrace, surrounding her with rags whose odor overpowered even the pot of fragrant spices. "I thought I was the last!" he exclaimed, his voice cracking. "I am overjoyed, overjoyed indeed."

"But—" began Kate, cringing at the potent smell.

"And we haven't had a woman join the Order since, my goodness! Since Katherine of Monmouth, ages ago."

Kate finally wriggled away. "What are you talking about?"

"You know, the Order of the Horn! The secret society dedicated to finding Merlin's Horn and delivering it to the Glass House, where it truly belongs."

She stared at him blankly.

"You have not heard of it?"

"And I'm not a member of it, either."

Geoffrey's bushy brows pinched together. "How cruel of you to mislead me."

"I didn't. You just assumed."

"If you didn't come here in search of the Horn, why did you come?"

She blinked. "By accident. I got thrown overboard."

Geoffrey observed her, toying with his beard. "And yet you know about the Horn."

"Not much, really. Just that lots of people have wanted it, for whatever reason. And whenever they find it, they lose it again."

Light returned to the deep-set eyes. "That is truer than you know. Merlin is only one of many who have sought it and been disappointed. Even that sorceress Nimue, for all her cleverness, has been frustrated."

"Nimue!"

The old man grimaced. "So you have heard of her. Let us hope that neither of us should ever have to meet her."

"You mean she's still around?"

"She is searching for the Horn, and nothing will stop her."

Sadly, Kate nodded. "My dad's in the same boat."

Geoffrey, looking perplexed, scratched the point of his nose. "But Nimue doesn't use a boat."

She rolled her eyes. "I mean, Dad's searching, too." Another wave of longing washed over her. "I wish I knew how to reach him. I'm sure he could help us."

"It is far easier to come here than it is to leave, I'm afraid. In fact, it's impossible as long as the whirlpool lasts. Yet if he is seeking the Horn, perhaps he will come here on his own."

"Before this whole place erupts, I hope." She considered what Geoffrey had said. "So the Horn . . . is really here?"

Geoffrey chewed some hairs for a moment, then said only, "It is near."

Kate edged a bit closer. "Is it the Horn that has kept you alive?"

"I cannot say for sure."

"You must have a theory," she pressed. "You've had five centuries to think about it."

"Well," he replied, "I have just a guess, nothing more."

"And?"

"My guess is that . . . the Horn keeps me from dying. Just as it keeps the whirlpool from collapsing and this ship from crumbling. Perhaps its power circulates with the swirling vapors here, passing into the very timbers and sails above our heads." He smacked his lips. "That would also explain why my dates remain so delightfully fresh."

Kate backed up a step. "And it would also explain Isabella's fish."

Confused again, Geoffrey asked, "Whose fish?"

"My friend Isabella's. The ugly old fish she found, the one with the wacky DNA chromosome. It should have been extinct."

Geoffrey studied her worriedly. "You're babbling, my dear. It's all been a bit much for you, hasn't it? You clearly need a nap."

"I'm fine," she replied tersely. "What else do you know about the Horn's power?"

At that instant a tremor rocked the ship, sending both of them sprawling. The walls swayed violently, creaking and popping. The tapestry tore loose and fell. With a crash, the porcelain dish shattered on the floor.

Then, silence. Plumes of dust swirled around the room. Geoffrey groaned painfully as he crawled to the chair.

Kate clambered to her feet. "Are you all right?"

"Barely," he replied. "Blast these tremors! Just look at my dates. Ruined! Covered with soot."

Kate squeezed the thin arm beneath the tattered clothes. "Listen to me. We've got to get out of here before a really big one hits."

"That could be centuries from now," groused Geoffrey. He plucked a date from the floor, blew the dust off it, and took a bite. "Right now I'm worried about more pressing matters."

"Like your dates," said Kate in disgust.

"Not wholly ruined," he observed, chewing slowly. "Pity about the dish, though."

"At least you could answer my question."

Geoffrey kept chewing. "Question?"

"Can you tell me anything else about the Horn's power? And is there some way we can use it to get out of here?"

Seemingly oblivious, Geoffrey inserted the rest of the date into his mouth. He removed the pit and threw it over his shoulder, but it caught on his tangle of hair and remained there, dangling.

"Delectable," he pronounced.

Kate demanded, "Come on. Tell me."

He gave her a sidelong glance. "Tell you what?"

"About the Horn!"

"Persistent, aren't you?" He crinkled his nose. "You remind me of another headstrong youth, one I understand Merlin found extremely difficult at times. His name was Arthur."

She drew a deep breath. "I don't care," she replied. "Answer me."

"Such stubbornness he had," mused Geoffrey. "Imagine,

thinking he could civilize the Saxons! The very idea he could teach them how to farm, convince them to join hands with other peoples instead of vanquishing them. Why, it's a wonder Merlin was able to keep him alive as long as he did. If that scoundrel Mordred hadn't . . ." The old man suddenly looked much older. "I do hope Merlin was right, though."

Caught off guard, Kate asked, "Right about what?"

"About Arthur," came the wistful reply. "That he will one day return."

His wrinkled hand reached under the chair for another date. Seeing this, Kate snatched it up and held it directly in front of his nose.

"Tell me," she demanded.

He reached for the date, but she yanked it away.

"It looks delicious," she said, twirling the sweet fruit in her fingers. "Soft, tender, juicy . . ."

"Please," he protested. "This is highly unfair."

"Tell me."

Geoffrey pulled anxiously at his beard. "I cannot! Not because I don't want to, but because I really don't know. No one knows. The precise nature of the Horn's power has remained a mystery, except to a few mer people—and the great Merlin himself, although that knowledge could not save him from his terrible end."

"Why all this secrecy?"

"Its power must be very great. Too great, perhaps." He started to stretch his hand toward the date.

Holding the precious item just out of reach, she queried, "Isn't there anything you *can* tell me?"

He shook his head, knocking the clinging date pit to the floor. "Only the riddle," he muttered.

"What riddle?"

"Merlin's own concoction. But it won't help, I can assure you. No one, not even a member of the Order of the Horn, has ever solved it. The only way to discover the power of the Horn is to drink from it! And that honor, as the Emperor Merwas long ago commanded, is reserved only for those with extraordinary wisdom and strength of will."

She tossed the date into the folds of his habit. "Tell me the riddle."

Geoffrey scooped it up, plunked it in his mouth, threw away the pit. Then he reached under his rags and scratched his chest vigorously. At length, he relented, and began to recite:

> *Ye who drink from Merlin's Horn*
> *May for dying not be mourned,*
> *May grow younger with the years,*
> *May remember ageless fears.*
>
> *Never doubt the spiral Horn*
> *Holds a power newly born,*
> *Holds a power truly great,*
> *Holds a power ye create.*

"*Holds a power,*" repeated Kate, deep in thought. She paced around the captain's quarters. "Holds a power *you* create? That doesn't make any sense."

Releasing another cacophonous yawn, Geoffrey slid lower in the chair. "You might try taking a nap. It might come to you while you sleep." He yawned again, his blackened teeth rattling. "Might just join you myself."

Without facing him, Kate said, "Merwas supposedly said

the Horn's power had something to do with eternal life. Is that true?"

Only a sputtering snore arose from the bundle of rags in the chair.

Ignoring him, she continued to pace, saying over and over what lines from the riddle she could remember. Yet the more she struggled, the more contradictory they seemed. Like pieces in a faulty jigsaw puzzle, they simply did not fit.

Glancing toward the snoring Geoffrey, she realized that she felt a bit drowsy herself. Maybe he was right, after all. Maybe a little rest would help. She would not allow herself to sleep, but at least she might be able to think more clearly.

Rounding the polished desk, she approached the thin bed by the wall. She pushed aside the roll of blankets and stretched out her body. Her sore back relaxed. She stared at the ancient timbers, working the riddle in her mind.

Soon she was breathing in time to Geoffrey.

XIV

UNINVITED GUEST

Cold. Blood chilling, bone-freezing cold. Biting enough to make Kate shiver. Aching enough to make her cry out in pain.

She awoke, shivering.

She grabbed the worn blanket at the base of the bed and pulled it over herself. It did no good. The bitter wind seemed to pass straight through the cover. Where did all that warm humidity go so suddenly?

Glancing at Geoffrey, she could see him snoring peacefully in the chair, apparently unaware of the extreme chill. Teeth chattering, she started to call to the old monk. But before she could utter a sound, something halted her.

A small shred of mist was forming in the window, curling over the sill like a sinewy finger. Yet this mist was darker, heavier, than any Kate had seen before. Through the window it snaked, stretching toward her.

Slowly, the dark finger flowed through the air to the edge of the desk. It oozed across the bronze astrolabe, through the twin handles of the gold cup, and around the slender red volume. Onward it moved, gradually approaching the bed where she clung to her blanket, transfixed.

She tried to scream, but she had no voice. She tried to rush from the bed to wake Geoffrey, but she had no strength. She felt helpless, caught in the icy grip of an irresistible power.

The flowing finger of mist stopped above the bed, hovering before her face. As she watched, it began to metamorphose. The mist condensed into the body of an infant, round and chubby, with an almost cherubic face. Clad in a graceful, silken robe, the infant hung in the air with no apparent effort. His full cheeks and gentle nose gave him a comforting, jovial appearance. Only the eyes, bright but deeply recessed, seemed oddly out of place.

As Kate stared in disbelief, the infant smiled at her kindly. Despite her shivering, she felt herself relax ever so slightly. At that moment a low, melodic laughter filled the room, and the infant's body shook with humor.

"You look cold," he purred. "Here, let me help you."

With that the infant blew upon Kate, and his breath was as warm as the desert sun. Her skin tingled, her muscles loosened, her heart expanded. Soon the chill wind had vanished. Cautiously, she allowed the blanket to slip from her shoulders.

"Thanks," she said hesitantly. "How did you do that?"

"It matters not," he replied in a soothing tone. "All you need to know is that I have come to protect you."

"And," she asked, dropping the blanket completely, "who are you?"

Again the infant smiled. "I am your friend. My magic is strong, and I am here to help you."

"Can you—can you help me get out of here?"

"If that is your desire."

"It is!" shouted Kate, so loud she was sure her cry would wake Geoffrey. Yet he slumbered on, slumped in the chair.

"Good." The hovering infant laughed, swaying with pleasure. "I will be happy to return you home."

"You can really do that?"

"With ease." The cherubic face beamed. "I need ask only one small favor in return."

"What favor?"

"I would like you to help me get . . . the Horn."

Astonished, Kate leaned closer. "The Horn of Merlin?"

"It does not belong to Merlin," said the infant, a hint of raspiness creeping into his voice. "It never did."

"But I don't have any idea where it is."

"You will." The soothing tone had returned. "I am sure you will."

She cocked her head. "If your magic is so strong, why can't you get it yourself?"

For a split second, the deep-set eyes glinted with something resembling anger. Then, just as swiftly, it passed. "I could, of course. But before I can help you, you must prove your worth."

"And what would you do with it?"

"I would simply . . . enjoy its power."

"Which is?"

"The power to live forever, of course."

Something about that definition did not seem quite right to Kate, but she was not sure what. "I don't think Geoffrey would like this idea."

"That old fool? You can disregard him. He is of no consequence." Floating in the air, the infant started circling the bed, as if tying a noose around her. "It is a simple matter, really. All you need to do is await my instructions."

Something about the way he said the word *instructions* made Kate feel a bit chilly again. She drew a deep breath and said, "I'm not sure. I'll have to think about it."

"Think about it?" snarled the infant. Then an aroma, sweet as apple blossoms, filled the room. The infant's eyes flamed once more, then began to sink deeper and deeper until finally they disappeared altogether, leaving only two holes, vacant as the void. At the same time, the cherubic face swelled into the face of a woman, whose long black hair fell over her shoulders. The rest of her body returned to mist, dark as smoke, with two wispy arms curling like tentacles. One of her vaporous hands brandished a blackened dagger.

Kate shrank back on the bed. A single word came to her, a word that chilled her anew. "Nimue."

"Yessss," said the enchantress, her voice like a jet of steam. "It issss I, or more precissssely, my image. For my body cannot yet passss through the wallssss of the whirlpool. Not yet, but ssssoon. Very ssssoon."

"What d-d-do you m-mean?" asked Kate, clutching the blanket again.

Nimue hissed in satisfaction. "You will ssssee. And if you do not help me, you will regret it."

"I w-won't," she said with effort.

"Then you will ssssuffer."

"Geoffrey!" she shrieked, shaking with cold. "Geoffrey, wak-ke up!"

The old man did not stir.

"He cannot hear you," declared Nimue, swimming lazily in the air above her. "Sssso lisssssten. I sssseek only one thing, and that issss the Horn. Whether you help me or not, I will get it. Of that I am ccccertain! For ssssome reasssson, though, I feel merccccciful today, enough to give you a ssssecond chancccce. If you assisssst me, I will sssspare your life."

Kate tried, without success, to stop shivering. "I w-w-will n-never help y-you."

"True?" spat Nimue. "I sssssuspect not. Here issss ssssomeone I shall ssssoon dessstroy, unless you change your mind."

The enchantress waved a misty hand. Another image, wavering in the dim light of the room, appeared beside her own. It was a face, one Kate recognized instantly.

"Dad!"

"Sssso you know him, do you? Then mark my wordssss. He issss my prissssoner."

"Let him go!" she wailed.

Nimue's mouth curled. "Hissss fate issss in your handssss."

The face of her father cringed, as if he were in pain. Kate herself cringed at the sight.

"All r-right," she answered in torment. "I will h-help you, if you p-p-promise not to harm him."

"Good choicccce," pronounced Nimue. "I will not harm him."

"P-promise?"

"I promisssse," said the enchantress, twirling her smoke-like form. "Now here issss what I assssk of you."

Raising one of her hands, Nimue swept it before Kate's face. A ring on one thin finger flashed with ruby light, so bright that it hurt her eyes.

"Look into my ring," Nimue commanded.

Kate averted her gaze, unwilling to do as she said.

Then the enchantress bellowed, "Look into my ring, or I will kill your father."

Biting her lip, Kate slowly lifted her head. The ruby light exploded in her eyes, but this time she did not turn away. All she could see was the powerful pulsing of the ring. All she could feel was its light burning into every corner of her brain.

"Very good," echoed the voice of the enchantress through the red fog that clouded Kate's vision. "That issss much better. I will give you no instructionssss now, but for thissss one command. Whenever you hear my voiccccce, wherever you may be, you will do only what I ssssay. Issss that understood?"

"Yes, Nimue," replied Kate slowly.

"Then let ussss tesssst your loyalty," the enchantress continued. "Raisssse your right arm, near to your mouth."

With stilted movements, Kate obeyed.

"Now bite your wrisssst. Hard."

Unable to resist, she clamped down her teeth on her own skin.

"Harder," ordered Nimue.

Kate bit fiercely, until a drop of blood swelled on her wrist and trickled down her arm.

"You may ceasssse," said Nimue, satisfied at last. As Kate lowered her arm, the enchantress declared, "You will not remember any of our meeting, nor any of our conversssssation. You will only remember my voiccccce, whenever you hear it. And that will be ssssoon. Very ssssoon."

Ruby light burst before Kate's eyes. Nimue disappeared, and with her, the cold.

XV
THE RED VOLUME

Kate awoke, more tired than when she had lain down to rest. Her mouth tasted strangely rancid, despite a lingering sweetness in the air. She stared at the glassless window, watching the vapors swirling outside, trying to recall a vague memory. Something about the window . . .

She rolled over, exhausted. It must be the constant half-light down here. How could Geoffrey ever sleep well, let alone keep track of the months and years? He had no sunrises and sunsets to guide him, no waxing and waning moon, no stars swimming overhead.

Besides, it was hot. Uncomfortably hot. Why did she have any need for a blanket? She threw aside her cover, then felt a piercing pain in her wrist.

Seeing the bloody wound on her skin, she gasped. Tearing a strip of cloth from the tail of her blue cotton shirt, she gingerly wrapped the injured arm. *Such a deep cut! Strange I don't remember getting it.* She paused before tying the bandage. Something else was odd about this cut, though she couldn't quite put her finger on it. It looked almost like . . . teeth marks. But of course that was impossible.

At that moment, Geoffrey yawned with the subtlety of a fog horn. Stretching his bony arms skyward, he shook his wild mane, scratched behind his neck, and, only then, opened his eyes.

"Yes," he crowed, "nothing like a good nap." He glanced her way. "Good morning to you, Miss Gordon."

"Call me Kate, all right?"

"Would you prefer Maid Kate?"

"Kate is fine."

The hawklike nose grew slightly pink. "My, such familiarity! As you wish, then. Good morning to you, Kate." With sudden concern, he added, "Why, you're wounded."

"I'm fine," she replied, trying the knot. "Just a scratch."

"Happens to me at least once a fortnight," consoled Geoffrey. "Did you find any success with the riddle?"

Kate merely frowned.

"Have a date, then." He picked one off the floor himself. "We shall eat something more substantial later. But first, I must practice my lessons."

"Lessons?"

Sliding the chair closer to the desk, he reached for the leather book. "A few of Merlin's gems, that's all. After centuries of practice, I have mastered only a few. Still, progress is progress."

Kate eyed the battered volume. "What is it, a magician's handbook?"

"You might call it that. It is a compendium of some of my mentor's wisdom, which I collected from learned sources over many years, then recorded in my own hand. Otherwise I could never remember any of it."

Cracking open the book, he paused at the first page, greeting it like an old friend. To Kate's surprise, the page was covered with slashes, curves, and crosses—the same secret language her father had spoken about. All except for six lines at the top, which were written in letters, but not words, she could recognize.

"What language is that?" she asked, pointing to the first six lines.

"Why, it's Latin, of course." Geoffrey looked at her askance. "Did you never go to school?"

"Sure," she answered. "I just, ah, missed Latin. What does it say?"

"Well," he sniggered, "it's my personal inscription. Books are precious, you know, so such things are customary."

"But what does it say?"

Geoffrey held the book closer. "My, such abominable handwriting," he muttered. "Even if it is my own."

Then he read:

> *The man who dares to steal this book*
> *Shall soon be hanged upon a hook,*
> *His entrails pulled, his liver cooked,*
> *His eyes gouged out, his backbone crook'd.*
> *For I would rather lose my purse,*
> *And he would rather die in curse.*

Lowering the book, he observed, "Rather makes the point, doesn't it?"

Kate gulped. "Rather."

He flipped through the pages, each one decorated with a small illustration at the top. After a time, he came to one showing a spoon with feathered wings.

"What's that?" asked Kate, pointing to the picture.

"Oh, that is the charm for levitation. One of the least useful but most entertaining ones in the book."

"Can you do it?"

"I can try," agreed the monk. "Let me see." He studied the page, mouthing some mysterious words to himself. Then he set down the book, pointed a long finger at the cooking pot of spices resting on the upturned barrel, and cleared his throat.

"Arzemy barzemy yangelo igg lom," he chanted.

Nothing happened.

Geoffrey pulled up his sleeve, cleared his throat again, and tried once more. *"Arzemy barzemy yangelo igg lom,"* he intoned. Quickly, he added, *"Abra cadabra."* Turning to Kate, he whispered, "That sometimes helps."

At that moment, the cooking pot quivered slightly. It slid toward the rim of the barrel. Then, with a slight crackling sound, it slowly lifted into the air, hovering a few inches above the barrel.

"You did it," said Kate in wonderment.

Geoffrey lowered his finger. The pot clattered back to its place, with a small amount of liquid sloshing over the top. He sighed wearily, but his dark eyes gleamed. "Just a little parlor trick, really."

"That's amazing! What else can you do?"

Geoffrey thumbed through the book, stopping at a page displaying an ant strolling beside an elephant. Underneath was a strange, convoluted design, surrounded by dozens of pictures of animals, plants, and constellations. "This is one of my favorites, the charm to change your shape. All you need to do is imagine very clearly what you want to become and say the proper words. Or, if you prefer, you can say nothing but concentrate deeply on this page, and something will happen."

His mouth twisted doubtfully. "Of course, it might not be what you *want* to happen." He slapped the side of his head.

"Drat those sea lice! As I was saying, these things can be tricky. The first time I tried to change myself into a robin, it was a bit too close to mealtime. My poor stomach rumbled just as I was concentrating, and I came out a rather spindly worm. Took me three whole days just to climb back up to the desk. Then I had to open the book again, which was no small feat for a worm."

Ignoring Kate's stifled laugh, he went on, "Still, it remains one of my most handy charms, as it was for Merlin himself. Do you know all the creatures he turned Arthur into? A fish, a hawk, a butterfly, a unicorn, and more. I find it oddly comforting to know that I can change myself into a totally different being any time I choose. Like starting life over, in a way." He sighed. "The difficult part is deciding just what I want to become."

He flipped to a page embroidered with intricate green-and-gold vines. "This one allows you to learn the languages of animals and plants. It has its pitfalls as well—Boar is perilously close to Camel, and Mosquito quite frankly gives me a headache—but it has proved invaluable to me. I have even used it to communicate with the whales."

"The gray whales?" asked Kate.

Geoffrey blinked his eyes slowly. "The ever-singing whales."

Kate spun her head toward the window. Somewhere out there, beyond the mist, beyond the whirling wall of water, swam those elusive creatures. She thought, with a pang, of the young whale she had tried to help. How long could he have survived with that severed tail? She would never know. Just as she would never know where and how her father was right now, although she could not suppress the uneasy feeling that something was wrong.

Without warning, the brass latch lifted and the door to the captain's quarters swung open. A large figure shadowed the doorway.

"Where the hell am I?" demanded a husky voice.

XVI
MAGMA

Kate's mouth went dry. "How did you get here?"

Turning sideways to fit through the door, Terry stepped inside. A swollen bruise marked his forehead, his glasses were gone, his Bermuda shorts hung ripped, and his entire body was smeared with wet sand.

"I'm the last one to answer that question," he muttered, leaning against the wall for support. "The boat, that storm . . . It happened so fast." He squinted at her. "I thought you were dead."

"No thanks to you, I'm not."

Terry looked down at his feet, started to say something, then caught himself. He thrust his chin at her. "You can't blame me because you fell overboard."

"I can blame you for not grabbing me when you had the chance," she retorted.

"I did what I could."

"Right."

Patting the bruise on his head, he winced. "I suppose you also blame me for what happened to the submersible."

The submersible. Suddenly it all came back to Kate. The hammer. The jammed lever. The cable releasing at last—from the wrong end.

"How could that happen?" she demanded.

Terry shrugged. "I have no idea. It wasn't supposed to happen, just as we weren't supposed to get thrown into the sea."

"But Dad and Isabella might be in danger! The submersible might be damaged or something."

"I doubt it. That thing is built to withstand a tidal wave. Probably has, more than once. Isabella must have had some way to release the cable from her side."

"Then why didn't she ever use it before? That doesn't add up."

"Look, quit the interrogation, will you? I know only as much as you do. They could be dead, for all I know."

"They're not!"

The geologist moved toward her, but clipped his thigh against the corner of the desk. "Ow! Where are my glasses?" Bending nearer, he asked hoarsely, "Are we the ones who are dead? I mean, this ship and all. It's ancient! A real museum piece. And, what's more, it's loaded to the gills with—"

"Treasure," completed the pile of brown rags on the chair.

Terry jolted. "What, er, who . . . are you?"

Creakily, the old man rose and extended a hand. "Geoffrey of Bardsey, at your service." He paused, looking confused, then asked, "Have we already been introduced?"

"And this is Terry Graham," said Kate, stepping to Geoffrey's side. "No need to kneel on his account."

"I'm hallucinating," moaned the broad-shouldered young man. "Or dead."

"You're not dead," declared Kate. "Not yet, anyway."

"Then where am I? Who is he?"

Facing him squarely, Kate replied, "You're on the *Resurrección*. Remember? The ship you said wasn't real. At the bottom of the whirlpool. And Geoffrey here is a survivor, kept alive somehow by a magical Horn. Is that enough for you?"

"Enough to convince me I'm crazy," said Terry uncertainly. "Wait. Did you say we're at the bottom of the whirlpool?"

Kate nodded.

"So that sand out there is really the ocean floor, three thousand feet down?"

Again she nodded.

"But . . . that isn't possible! Look, be rational. It's so warm here. Too warm for that far down. Unless . . ." His eyes bulged. "Have you felt any tremors?"

"More than one."

Terry went pale. "Then, if this is the ocean floor, magma must be pushing closer! There could be an eruption any moment." He waved at the air. "And we're stuck down here. Hopelessly stuck."

Sensing his anxiety, she felt an unexpected touch of sympathy. "Maybe not."

"Hopeless is an unfortunate state of mind," offered Geoffrey. "It is very difficult, while feeling hopeless, to remain at all, well, hopeful."

Kate and Terry traded perplexed looks. Then Kate asked the monk, "Are you absolutely sure there is no way the Horn could help us?"

"Not unless you can solve the riddle."

"Tell me what else you know about the Horn," she insisted. "Maybe it will give me a clue."

Geoffrey regarded her doubtfully. "I suppose I could tell you a story I learned during my time in the Order of the Horn—the story of how the Horn came to be found, and then lost, by Merlin. Beyond that, all I can tell you is how, long after Merlin's demise, I came to find it again."

"Go ahead," she pleaded.

"I really would rather—"

"Please."

Geoffrey cracked his withered knuckles. "I never could say no to the ladies," he muttered. "All right. It is, I admit, an intriguing tale. One of hope and promise."

He reached for the red volume, tucked it under his arm, then started hobbling toward the door. As he passed Kate, he remarked, "The deck is the place to do it, though. Out with the sails and the fresh air."

Reluctantly, Kate and Terry followed.

Geoffrey led them onto the deck, past the rows of cannons and the cases of cannonballs and bar shot. Near the trapdoor, he stopped and lifted a rammer off the deck. Reaching as high as he could, he used the rammer to tip over a round clay jar lashed to the rigging above his head. A brief cascade of water, collected from the constant vapors of the whirlpool, poured onto his upturned face. Then he shook himself, cast the rammer aside, and tottered onward.

His version of a shower, thought Kate. *All he needs now is some shampoo. Strong enough to kill lice.*

At the base of the snapped mainmast, the monk stepped over a tangle of rigging and sat down on a broken barrel. Motioning to the others to join him, he looked up into the swirling clouds of mist, as if searching for a glimpse of the blue sky he had not seen for half a millennium.

Kate sat on the dark wood of the deck before him, leaning

her back against the side of a crate. As Terry joined her, he grumbled, "Do you really expect to learn anything useful from this character?"

"Got any better ideas?" she replied.

"No." He gingerly wiped the salty dew from his brow. "But every minute we sit here the eruption gets closer."

Geoffrey tilted his haggard face toward them. He scratched behind his knee and between two toes, then intoned, "Our story begins in the age of Merlin, long after Arthur perished at the hands of Mordred."

Terry released a painful groan, causing Kate to elbow him.

"Merlin learned of a legendary craftsman, whose life was steeped in tragedy. He lived all alone, high on a mountain precipice. His true name had been lost from memory, but he was known as—"

"Emrys," finished Kate.

Geoffrey and Terry both looked at her with surprise, though the elder's expression showed a touch of admiration, as well.

"You are correct," said Geoffrey. "Now may I continue?"

"Yes."

"Oh, by the way. When I come to the part concerning me—how I came to find the Horn—I will speak of myself as Geoffrey. That is because . . . this is how, long after my time has passed, I hope the story will be told."

He squared his shoulders. "Now listen well, for you shall learn how Serilliant came to be . . . the Horn of Merlin."

XVII

The Story of the Whirlpool's Birth

When King Arthur died, the wizard Merlin's hopes for peace and justice in *Clas Myrddin* died as well. His only scant comfort came from the prophesy that one day, under certain conditions, Arthur might return. The prophesy told of a Final Battle that would follow where Arthur would fight against all the assembled forces of wickedness. If Arthur won, the world would be liberated, but if he lost, the world would sink into chaos and despair.

Merlin believed that the Thirteen Treasures created by Emrys would be essential to Arthur in that colossal battle. Merlin's friends, the elusive mer people, had told him enough about the Horn named Serilliant to convince him that it was the most valuable of all the Treasures. Yet they would not reveal, even to Merlin, the secret of its power. They warned him that the Horn must never fall into the hands of Arthur's enemies, or his cause would surely be doomed.

After years of searching, Merlin finally discovered the mountain hideaway of Emrys. Merlin found the craftsman on the verge of death, still tormenting himself for the loss of his one true love, the mermaid Wintonwy. Although Merlin could do nothing to relieve Emrys' pain, he convinced him to contribute the Treasures to the cause of Arthur. So Emrys gave Merlin the flaming chariot, the cauldron of knowledge, the mantle of invisibility, the knife that could heal any wound, and the other Treasures in his possession. But he could not deliver the three that had been lost: the sword of light, the ruby ring that could control the will of others, and—most precious of all—the mysterious Horn.

Guided by the directions Emrys provided, Merlin made his way to the realm of Shaa. At last he came to the entrance. There he found a fearsome monster of the deep, a spidery creature with a thousand poisonous tongues. By the monster's side lay the sword of light. Merlin hid himself and waited until the moment the monster began to doze. Then, changing his own form into a small crab, Merlin managed to spirit away the sword of light.

After passing through an abyss, darkest of the dark, Merlin entered the realm of Shaa. It lay, as legend described, in *the place where the sea begins, the womb where the waters are born.* No mer people remained there, having abandoned the realm after Nimue's brutal attack. And, as Merlin had hoped, Nimue and her army of sea demons had also left, having found nothing more in Shaa to steal or destroy. Even the ancient castle of Merwas stood vacant, its great hall drained of water and of life.

Merlin searched relentlessly for the two Treasures still missing. Yet he could find no clue to their whereabouts. Finally, near the forgotten castle, the wizard happened upon an enormous pile of discarded conch shells. All were spiral in shape, all were empty—but for one, which seemed to glisten strangely. Out of curiosity, Merlin retrieved it, only to realize that it brimmed with a rainbow-colored fluid. He knew in a flash that he had recovered the lost Serilliant. Triumphant, he returned to the land above the sea.

Only those whose wisdom and strength of will are beyond question may drink from this Horn. Merlin knew well this command, yet he found himself increasingly consumed by his desire to experience the Horn's power. He believed that his vast wisdom would surely pass the test, and would no doubt make up for any deficiencies in his strength of will. In time, he ignored his own better judgment and decided that Arthur would want him to take a drink from the Horn.

And then he drank. His eyes flamed with a newfound brightness. Yet because he had not waited to drink from the Horn until his strength of will was greater, he began to grow possessive and arrogant, more so with each passing day.

Telling himself that no one but himself, perhaps not even Arthur, could fully appreciate the Horn's power, Merlin carried it with him wherever he went. Before long he stopped calling it Serilliant and started referring to it as the Horn of Merlin. Though it came to be no less part of his garb than his fabled blue cloak, he steadfastly refused to divulge to anyone, even his closest friends, the nature of its power.

While under the sea, Merlin had discovered an ideal place to store the Treasures until the return of Arthur. This place was far from Britain, deep beyond imagining, and almost impossible to find. Merlin called it the Glass House. He kept its location secret, although from time to time he hinted that it lay hidden beneath the waves. In time, he brought all the Treasures to the Glass House for safekeeping. All, that is, except the ruby ring, which he had not yet found, and the Horn itself, which he could not bear to leave behind.

Merlin traveled widely, with the Horn ever at his side. In his arrogance, he flaunted it, believing that the Horn was destined to remain with him always. No one, he told himself, would be so foolish as to try to steal it.

He was wrong. The sorceress Nimue had long envied Merlin. She had often tried, with limited results, to trick him into parting with his secrets. Realizing that the Horn could confer unrivaled power, she vowed that she would one day possess it. Then, at last, she would be greater than Merlin, greater than anyone who might dare to challenge her.

Carefully, Nimue crafted a plot. It was founded on the belief that, one day, Merlin would choose to return to the Glass House under the sea to inspect the Treasures hidden there. To succeed, she knew she would need an ally, one who would not shy away from a great battle on the open ocean.

She sought out a certain sea captain, a man named Garlon. Such great distances had he sailed that it was said that neither war nor weather could sink a ship if Garlon the Seaworthy stood at the helm. For some reason known to no one but Garlon himself, he seethed with contempt for Merlin. Nimue knew not the origins of his hatred, but she knew well how to fan its embers into flames. She approached Garlon aboard his ship one day, enticing him with her sweet perfume and her promises of wealth beyond measure. But these meant less to him than the chance he had longed for, the chance to humble Merlin at last. He agreed to help.

For a long time, Nimue waited. At length, the desired day arrived. Disguised as a cloud of mist upon the water, she watched as Merlin readied a barge drawn by a great whale. The wizard boarded the barge, then commanded the whale to take him to *the place where the sea begins, the womb where the waters are born.*

As the barge drew farther away from Britain, mysterious winds seemed to gather around it, driving it toward a faraway destination. Unnoticed, the sorceress followed at a distance. Hidden behind her curtain of mist, Garlon sailed his own ship, propelled by the same winds that drove Merlin.

Finally, the winds ceased. Merlin released the whale and prepared to plunge beneath the waves. At that instant, Nimue cast aside her disguise. She attacked the lone wizard, joined by her band of sea demons and the vengeful Garlon.

Although he had no army to defend him, Merlin held his own for some time. The battle raged on for weeks, turning night into day and water into fire. But in time, the combined forces against him proved too strong. Merlin realized that he could not prevail. In that bitter moment, he also understood his own colossal folly. He had broken the command of Merwas; he had wasted his opportunity to protect the Horn; he had betrayed the very cause of his king.

As Nimue and Garlon bore down on him, Merlin tried to think of some way to save the Horn, even if he could not save himself. In desperation, he hurled the Horn as far as he could from the attackers.

Nimue merely laughed, gloating in triumph. "Do you think you can sssstop me sssso eassssily?"

Then, as the Horn hit the water, something remarkable occurred. As it started spiraling downward into the depths, the Horn caused the water to start spinning around it. Soon the ocean itself began whirling with ever-greater force, and a dark hole opened on the surface of the sea.

A great whirlpool was born.

Seizing his chance, Merlin mustered all his remaining power. He cast a protective spell over the whirlpool, so that only those who were friends of King Arthur—or Arthur himself—could enter the whirlpool and survive.

Nimue tried to force her way into the mouth of the whirlpool but could not. She exploded in rage. Merlin had denied her the Horn! She swooped down on the exhausted wizard and carried him away, dropping him into a deep cave on the Isle of Bardsey, which she sealed forever.

Yet, so great was Nimue's desire for the Horn, she could not accept defeat. She returned to the whirlpool, determined to wait until it finally slowed and collapsed, no matter how long that might take. After all, there was now no risk of being menaced by Merlin. In exploring the area below the whirlpool, she discovered Merlin's Glass House. She claimed it for her own, although its store of Treasures held no interest for her. The one Treasure she most wanted lay beyond her reach . . . for the moment.

Nimue took Garlon, against his will, to the Glass House under the sea. Although he had no desire for the Horn, he had been useful to her once, and might be so again. Yet he resisted serving as her underling, even as he resisted living deep under the waves. Once he tried to escape to the surface and was apprehended by her sea demons.

Though the sea demons wanted to tear Garlon to shreds, Nimue halted them. Instead, she raised her vaporous hand and laid on him a terrible curse. *If Garlon should ever again go above the surface of the sea, he would instantly disintegrate and perish—unless he had first taken a drink from the Horn.* Thus Garlon's loyalty was ensured, for unless he could somehow recover the Horn, he would never again feel the touch of sunlight on his skin.

Years passed, turning into decades, then into centuries. Still the whirlpool persisted, surrounded in time by a group of whales, singing and circling without end. All this time Nimue waited, with Garlon at her side, kept alive by the power of the Horn that seeped through the whirlpool into the surrounding waters. Yet she had not counted on the fact that the Horn would also nourish the whirlpool and keep it spinning strongly—so strongly that it showed no sign of ever collapsing. While she suspected that the whirlpool's strength would prevent any friend of Arthur who might get in from ever getting out again, she also began to fear that her vigil might be prolonged forever.

Unknown to Nimue, on the one thousandth anniversary of Merlin's demise, the spirit of the great wizard appeared in the dream of Geoffrey of Bardsey, the last surviving member of the Order of the Horn.

"Last of the faithful," the spirit of Merlin declared, "I come to you with a command."

"Are you sure?" asked Geoffrey in protest. "I am rather weak and frail."

The spirit examined the aging monk with evident disappointment. "You are the only one I have left. For one thousand years I have slept in constant torment, not knowing whether the Horn could still be saved for Arthur. Yet now, through the whispering of mer folk who come near my cave, I have learned that there is indeed a thin strand of hope. But I need your assistance."

The spirit of Merlin then told Geoffrey all that had befallen the Horn. He concluded with this command: "Go now to the distant port of Manila. There you will find, preparing to sail, a ship known as *Resurrección*. You must smuggle yourself aboard, then ride with the ship, wherever it may go. For its route will take you close to the mighty whirlpool where the Horn lies to this very day."

Geoffrey scratched his neck nervously. "Surely you are not expecting me to sail into the mouth of a whirlpool."

The spirit scowled at him, then said only, "The ship will lead you to the Horn."

With that, the spirit disappeared and Geoffrey of Bardsey awoke. Despite his fears, not to mention his tender feet, he made his way across Asia to Manila. He arrived just as the ship was being loaded with priceless treasures. He boarded and hid himself away, but not before he made a small coded entry in the ship's manifest, on the remote chance that it might one day alert an ally who could somehow provide assistance.

Soon after the ship was launched, Geoffrey discovered its generous stores of food. Finding himself eating better than ever before in his life, he began to conclude that his original fears had been misplaced. Surely Merlin would never reward his loyalty by causing him to plunge into a deadly whirlpool!

Months passed at sea, and Geoffrey began to wonder whether he would ever see the hills of his home again. Then came a morning when the ship suddenly changed course, spinning in ever tighter circles. Sailors started cursing and howling like wounded beasts. Geoffrey rushed out to the deck to discover that the ship was, indeed, being swallowed by the whirlpool. Men screamed in fright and leaped overboard into the churning waves, even as wind tore at the sails and the mainmast snapped in two.

Just as he uttered his final prayers, Geoffrey heard the men crying that they were being devoured by whales. Then, to his astonishment, he saw that they were in truth being saved, carried to shore before they could drown.

Alas, the whales did not seem at all interested in saving Geoffrey. Though he called to them, waved his arms wildly, and begged to be taken in their jaws, they paid no attention to him. So one man, and one man alone, went down with the doomed ship.

XVIII
AGELESS FEARS

Geoffrey hung his head dejectedly. "And here I have stayed."

"I wish my dad could have heard that," said Kate. "But I thought you were going to tell a story of hope and promise."

The old man pouted. "I suppose I exaggerated a bit."

"A bit! I feel more hopeless than ever."

"Enough sitting around," announced Terry, pushing to his feet. "I'm going out there to see if I can learn anything useful."

"Be careful," warned Kate.

"Don't go too far," added Geoffrey.

"Do I have any choice?" The young man gestured at the whirling wall of water surrounding the ship. He strode off, stumbled on a warped timber, then lifted the trapdoor and descended.

Watching him, Geoffrey sighed. "Impatient youth! Though I can't suppose I blame him for wanting to try to find a way out of here. But with the whirlpool's strength intensified by the Horn, no one—not even a great magician—could escape."

"How did he get in, anyway? You said that only a friend of Arthur could enter the whirlpool."

Thoughtfully, Geoffrey tugged his beard. "I cannot say. Perhaps time will tell."

"I wish I could talk to Dad," Kate said wistfully. "He'd have an idea . . . unless he's in too much trouble himself right now."

"Tell me," probed the monk. "Just what would your father do if he were here?"

"He'd think. About where we might find a clue. The way he did with the ballad."

"Ballad?"

Kate pursed her lips. "It's an old ballad about the ship, the whirlpool, the whales. I can't remember much, but it ends in the weirdest way:

> *One day the sun will fail to rise,*
> *The dead will die,*
> > *And then*
> *For Merlin's Horn to find its home,*
> *The ship must sail again.*"

"Weird, indeed," agreed Geoffrey, studying her with keen interest. "Especially that part about Merlin's Horn finding its home." He swatted at a strand of rigging dangling by his head. "Can't make hide nor hair of it, I'm afraid."

"Maybe the Horn's home is wherever it is now." She returned his scrutiny. "You do know where it is, don't you? How did you find it, anyway?"

"Stubbed my toe on it, to be precise. It was practically buried in the sand near the anchor."

"Have you ever . . . taken a drink from it?" asked Kate, her voice a whisper.

"No," he replied. "You recall what happened to Merlin when he took a drink before he had passed the test of Mer-was, don't you? He lost whatever good sense he had! And before long, he lost everything else as well. That's not to say that I haven't been tempted. I have. Often."

"You must have plenty of willpower to resist."

"Not really. I'm as weak as any mortal being. Weaker, no doubt. But I do have one advantage that poor Merlin never had. The whirlpool surrounding this ship seems to coax out the essence of the Horn, and I breathe some of it in these swirling vapors every day. That has to ease my thirst a bit, although it is not the same as drinking from it directly."

A bit guiltily, he added, "On top of that, I sometimes allow myself to sniff the Horn's aroma, just to smell that fragrance of the mountaintop that Emrys gave to it."

"Do you do that often?"

The hint of a grin touched Geoffrey's face. "Only on Feast Days and Holy Days. Of course, there are dozens and dozens of those! Last time was the Sunday after Saint Vitus' Day."

Staring into the mist off the bow, Kate said darkly, "If your story is true, while we're trying to find some way to pass through the whirlpool, so is Nimue."

At the mention of that name, Kate felt a cold wind blow over the deck of the *Resurrección*. She shivered and turned to Geoffrey. Oddly, he did not seem to have noticed anything. Her chill soon passed, yet it left her with the uncomfortable feeling that she had felt it before, and would, before long, feel it again.

The old man patted her arm. "That wretched sorceress craves nothing more than the chance to drink from the Horn. But for several centuries now, we've had something of a stalemate, she and I. She can't get into the whirlpool, and I can't get out! The wall that divides us is utterly impermeable. So you needn't worry. Nimue and her sea demons, along with Garlon, have been trying for ages to get in here, with no luck. Why should anything be different now?"

"She must be getting awfully impatient."

He angled his face upward. "If it makes you feel any better, on top of Merlin's protective spell, we have the whales."

"The gray whales?"

Geoffrey nodded. "They seem to work very hard at keeping intruders away from the whirlpool. And, similarly, the ship."

Kate reflected on this. Could the whales, as Isabella suspected, have purposely tried to erase the sonic image of the sunken ship? Could the whale who was so badly tangled at the buoy have been trying to interfere with the equipment?

"Why would they do that?" she demanded.

"At first, perhaps, it was their old loyalty to Merlin. But in more recent times, they mainly want to keep people away from themselves."

"What makes you say that?"

He scratched vigorously inside each of his nostrils, then lifted the slender red volume. "They told me so themselves. I can listen to them whenever I like, with this."

Kate slid closer. "Your little red book?"

"Haven't done it much lately," he continued, trying to stifle a yawn. "This infernal heat, you know. Makes me sleep more than usual. But in times past I have listened to the whales for hours on end. Because their hearing is so good, they have become the ocean's eavesdroppers. I have even listened to the songs of the whales who don't stay by the whirlpool year after year, who swim every year to the far north. From them I have learned about the coldness of currents, the size of newborns, the passage of seasons, the taste of krill, the motions of stars."

"You were saying that the whales want to keep people away."

A cloud passed over Geoffrey's face. "Once, long ago, the whales befriended everyone, just as they did Merlin. They were as helpful to him as the mer people—more so, because they were not so difficult to find. Ever since the fall of the realm of Shaa, mer folk have lived in the shadows, appearing only rarely. Not so the whales. In Merlin's day, and even in mine, they felt no reason to hide. So they had no hesitation about showing themselves to save the sailors from the *Resurrección*. I am sorry to say they paid dearly for that mistake."

"How?"

"Word spread. Hunters came in droves. Soon only a few whales remained alive. Some of the survivors simply swam away, never to return. Others chose to stay in these waters near the whirlpool, circling endlessly, grieving for their lost mothers and fathers, sisters and brothers. Still others chose to swim to the far north, hoping to evade more hunters by moving always, never resting. They are the lucky ones, because they have grown old and died, making room for new generations who are not burdened by such painful memories."

At once, Kate understood. "So that is why the songs of the whales who stay around here are so sad."

"Right. The nearness of the Horn sustains them somehow, as it does the ship, the whirlpool, and myself. But for them, continuing to live means continuing to suffer. Their fate is most cruel. They cannot forget, cannot move on.

> *Ye who drink from Merlin's Horn*
> *May for dying not be mourned*
> *May grow younger with the years*
> *May remember ageless fears.*"

Kate thought again of the young whale ensnared in the net. Had he been more afraid of drowning, or of her? She ran her hand along a length of rigging, sturdy as it was when it left Manila centuries ago.

Geoffrey looked at the vapors swimming about the sails. "It is said, by the whales themselves, that their agony will not be over until the whirlpool itself comes to an end."

At that, the trapdoor flew open. Terry squeezed through the opening up to his armpits. "A steam vent!" he exclaimed, his voice full of fear. "Opened up right by my feet, not far from the hull."

"Steam, eh?" asked Geoffrey calmly. "No wonder it's so beastly hot."

"Don't you see?" the geologist cried. "The eruption is going to happen any time now! We're all going to be burned to ashes, including your precious Horn."

Geoffrey's wrinkles deepened. "My, my! That *is* rather worrisome."

"Worrisome! Can't you understand, old man? This isn't going to be just another tremor. This is going to be a full-scale eruption!"

Geoffrey shook his head. "But I don't understand how such a thing could happen. The Horn ought to be protecting us, as it has these many years. Something must have changed! I only wish I knew what."

Kate seized him by the shoulder. "The whales might know! You said they hear all kinds of things. Try listening to them!"

"An excellent idea," agreed the monk.

"A ridiculous idea," countered Terry.

"Come on," said Kate, taking Geoffrey's arm to help him stand. "Let's try it."

Opening the book to the page decorated with green-and-gold vines, Geoffrey inhaled deeply, then began to concentrate on the page. At once, the continuous humming of the whirlpool reduced to a mere whisper. All other sounds, including their own breathing, diminished. At the same time, one sound grew steadily louder, until it seemed to spring from only inches away.

The wailing rose and fell like the surging waves. Kate could not tell just how many whales were singing, only that some of the voices sounded young and vibrant, others old and thin. All of them exuded sorrow.

She glanced at Geoffrey, who was scratching his ear anxiously. All of a sudden, he stopped. His hand fell to his side. For a long moment he stood as still as a wax figure.

Finally, the ragged robes stirred. At the same time, the mournful cries of the whales receded until, at last, they could no longer be heard.

Geoffrey grasped a line of rigging to steady himself. His face a mixture of fear and confusion, he mumbled, "It can't be so."

"What did they say?" pressed Kate.

"They said," he replied, almost choking on the words, "that Nimue has finally lost her patience. That she has set out . . . to destroy the whirlpool."

"But how?"

From the corner of her eye, Kate saw Terry lean forward to hear better.

"She has found some way to make the rock beneath the ocean floor buckle and boil. Until . . . until it explodes like a volcano."

"The eruption," whispered Terry.

Kate tugged Geoffrey's robe. "Where is Nimue now?"

"Still in the Glass House, not far from here."

"But wouldn't the eruption destroy that, too? And all the Treasures there?"

"Nimue cares not! If somehow she can shatter the whirlpool and escape with the one thing she craves more than any other, that is her only goal."

"Wait a minute," objected Terry. "I'm the first to agree we're on the edge of an eruption. But . . . this is *geological force* we're talking about. Primal. Uncontrollable. Even if you accept the idea of a sorceress and her sea demons, which I don't, they couldn't control volcanic energy. Nothing can! And besides, why would anyone want to do something like that?"

Geoffrey examined him grimly. Then he reached one hand deep into the folds of his habit. He seemed to be searching for something, or possibly scratching again. Then, slowly, he pulled out his hand—and a gleaming object, suspended from a necklace of scarlet coral beads. Shaped like a curling conch shell, it glistened with a sheen of blue and silver. Within its mouth brimmed fluid no less radiant than a rainbow.

"This is why," he announced.

Kate stared in awe at the Horn.

Terry pulled himself through the trapdoor and came over for a closer look. Like Kate, he kept looking at the wondrous object, which glowed with an opalescent luster.

She reached to stroke its smooth surface with one finger. Quietly, she said, "They're all the same shape, aren't they?"

"What are?" asked Geoffrey.

"The Horn, the secret code, the whirlpool. They're all a spiral."

"Yes," agreed the monk, a curious gleam in his eye. "So they are."

"Let me get this straight," said Terry. "You're saying

this—this sorceress of yours is trying to cause an eruption just so she can get that thing."

"Precisely."

"Are you sure you heard the whales say that?"

"Quite sure," Geoffrey answered. "They were perfectly clear." He replaced the Horn under his garment. "The only questionable part came at the end."

"What was that?"

"I hesitate to tell you, since I might have misunderstood."

"Tell us," Kate insisted.

"All right. It seems Nimue has taken some unfortunate souls as her prisoners." He swatted the side of his neck. "That may or may not be true, but the puzzling part is that the whales described the prisoners' ship as, well, an enormous bubble."

"A what?"

"Quite absurd, I agree. Imagine a ship built like a bubble."

"I can! It's my dad!"

The wooly eyebrows lifted. "Your father? Are you sure?"

"Yes!"

"I am sorry to hear that. Dreadfully sorry."

Looking from Geoffrey to Terry, Kate cried, "We've got to do something!" She grabbed the monk by the shoulders. "Isn't there any way we can get out of here while the whirlpool is still going?"

His dark eyes seemed to darken even more. "No. I told you, the whirlpool is impermeable. No creature of flesh could survive the passage."

"But *something* must be able to pass through it!" She glanced at the whirling spiral of water. "You said yourself the power of the Horn seeps through somehow. How else could it affect the whales?"

Geoffrey jolted as if he had been struck with a hammer. "You might . . . be onto something. Yes, yes . . . you just might." Pensively, he combed his beard with his fingers. "I am not sure it will work, but . . . there could, in fact, be a way. I am stunned that in all the time I've been here I never thought of it before."

"What is it?"

"It will be risky. Very risky. I would not try it at all, except that the Horn, and all the other Treasures, are in such grave danger. Everything Merlin worked so hard to achieve, everything he did to aid Arthur, is at stake."

"Dad's *life* is at stake!" Kate shook him fiercely. "You've got to take me with you."

He pulled free. "I am sorry," he said firmly. "It will be dangerous enough for one person to go. As it is, I have no idea how to stop Nimue. I only know I must try."

"I can help you," she pleaded.

"I may be a fool," he replied, shaking his head, "but I am not that much of a fool. As unsafe as you may be here, you are safer here than going with me. Even if I can somehow survive the whirlpool, the route to the Glass House, which I know only from the whales, is fraught with dangers and darkness." His furrowed face filled with compassion. "I will do what I can to help your father."

"Take me with you. Please."

A sudden tremor rocked the ship. Geoffrey shouted, tumbling backward into a maze of rigging. Terry skidded across the deck, smashing a row of clay jars. As timbers splintered and buckled, the floorboards under Kate gave way. She fell through a hole, landing on a mound of bundles in the darkened deck below.

With a final shudder, the violent quaking ceased.

Struggling to gain her bearings, Kate rubbed her sore neck.

She crawled over the bundles to the wooden ladder and rapidly scaled the rungs. Seconds later, she burst out of the trapdoor onto the main deck.

Pulling Terry loose from a web of torn rigging, she helped him to his feet. Then, as if one, their eyes trained on the spot where Geoffrey had stood only a moment before.

He had vanished.

XIX

SWIRLING VAPORS

Where did he go?" asked Kate.

"Beats me," Terry muttered.

She ran over to the mainmast. The old man was nowhere to be seen. Picking up a cannonball at her feet, she hefted it like a shot-put.

Where had he gone? Her neck stung, her back ached. Yet those things did not trouble her nearly as much as the disappearance of her prime companion in this strange undersea world. Despite his bizarre manner, she had found herself almost liking Geoffrey. He reminded her a little of her own grandfather, eccentric and vulnerable, or maybe of someone she had known in a story, or a dream. No matter. He was gone.

In frustration, she hurled the cannonball into the mass of rigging at the base of the broken mast. Then an idea drifted into her thoughts. Maybe he, too, had fallen through the floor! Maybe even now he lay sprawled on some stack of crates on a lower deck. She started shoving the rigging aside, searching for another hole in the deck.

Without a word, Terry came over and started helping. Although he was a bit clumsy without his glasses, he was strong enough to heave aside cases and timbers that she could barely budge.

After several minutes of furious searching, she concluded it was useless. Panting, she crumpled onto a barrel and sat there, her head in her hands.

Terry straightened up stiffly. Delicately wiping his sore brow, he said, "No sign of him."

Kate lifted her head. "No. Thanks for helping, anyway."

"Sure." He leaned against the mast. "Don't know where he could have gone."

Her gaze fell on the jumble of rigging, and suddenly it came to her. "I do. He's gone to stop Nimue."

"But how?"

"He said there was a way."

Terry kicked away a piece of bar shot. "He must be part fish, then. And even so, he couldn't survive the whirlpool. Can you imagine the pressure of that water, with the strength to hold back half a mile of ocean? It's probably several thousand pounds per square inch." He studied the swirling vapors. "No, not unless the whirlpool slowed way down, for whatever reason, could anything pass through it and survive."

Stubbornly, Kate threw her braid over her shoulder. "Then where is Geoffrey? He found a way."

"I'll give him this," said Terry. "If he did find a way, he's plenty ingenious. Not to mention self-sacrificing." His shoulders drooped a notch. "I guess you already found out how self-sacrificing I am."

She turned to him, saw the regret in his eyes. "Up there on the *Skimmer?* Look, you wanted to grab me. You just didn't move fast enough."

"No way. I was more concerned about my equipment than anything else. I might not have saved you, but at least I could have tried. Really tried."

Kate scrutinized him. "If that's an apology, I accept. Now let's get back to finding some way out of here. Maybe the whirlpool has a weak point."

"Don't kid yourself. Lousy as it is, our only sane option is to stay put. There's a tiny chance we could survive an eruption. But there's zero chance we could survive the whirlpool."

"It's not the eruption I'm worried about. It's my dad! And Isabella! I can't just sit here and do nothing."

Terry shook his head. "Keep your wits, will you? This is real, not just a story in some book."

Kate sat upright. "That's it. The little red book!"

She rushed to the mainmast and retrieved the slender volume lying at its base. "He used this!"

"Come off it," scoffed Terry. "Talking with animals is one thing. Disappearing into thin air is another."

Madly, she flipped the pages to the one displaying an elephant and an ant. "This must be it! What did Geoffrey say to do? Either say all the magic words, or just look at the design and . . . concentrate. Hard."

Clenching her jaw, she started to imagine herself as a deep-water fish. Like the one Isabella bought from the fisherman. She stared at the page, then suddenly halted herself.

That wouldn't work. Terry was right. No fish could withstand the pressure of the whirlpool wall. What had Geoffrey said? *No creature of flesh could survive.* Even a piece of eight would probably not last.

She chewed her lip. What was it she had said that gave Geoffrey his idea? That the power of the Horn, somehow, gets through . . .

"Give up," advised Terry.

"There has to be a way!"

Following the curling clouds of vapor with her eyes, she considered the puzzle. She tried to recall Isabella's theory of how *the Merlin effect* might work. Some kind of particle that circulates in the water, altering the genes. Circulating. Water.

Water! That was the answer. Something more like water than like flesh might be able to get through. How had Isabella described those early single-celled creatures? *More water than organism.*

She closed her eyes, fixing her thoughts on the idea of water, vaporous and elusive, without shape or substance, rising softly through the air. Then, opening her eyes, she did her best to hold the image in her mind and stare at the page without blinking.

Nothing. She concentrated harder, holding the book before her face. Water being. Water creature. *Water spirit.*

Just then, Terry snatched the book from her hands.

"Give that back," she cried, wrestling with him. "I need it!"

Holding the book just beyond her reach, he crooned, "When in doubt, try hocus pocus." He gestured wildly and said in his deepest voice, "I am Ali Baba Heebee Jeebee, the great magician."

"Give it back!" she bellowed, finally getting her hand on the volume. She tried to pull it away from him. "I've almost got it right."

"Have you tried this?" he asked, pretending to sweep a cape across his shoulders. *"Abra cadabra!"*

There was a nearly inaudible *pop*, just as the book dropped to the deck. No one picked it up again.

XX
WATER SPIRIT

Before feeling came memory.

Vague as reflections in a pool, wispy as visions in the mist, the first memories drifted to Kate. The many forms of water flowed in and around her. She remembered all she had been and might yet become. She yearned to begin again.

I am rain. Showering, sprinkling, misting, pouring. Rolling with thunder, pulsing with light. I scatter the sun, each droplet a prism, connecting soil and sky with archways of color. To soak, to fill, that is what I am about. To find every last thirsty thing and give it new life. I sparkle as I weep. For I am made to dance, even as I cry.

I am stream. Bright and bouncy rivulet, born of mountain snows, cascading through a meadow. Cold on the tongue. Brimming with sunshine. Splash, trickle, lap, gurgle. Over the rock, under the spout, down the channel. Call me *creek* in Colorado, *burn* in Scotland, *wadi* in Egypt, *arroyo* in Spain, *billabong* in Australia. I link summits to seas, freshets to rivers. I seek, I surge, I murmur and purl. And I never rest, I never stop.

I am ice. Smooth and sharp, gripping and binding. Ever so slowly I spread and harden, over lakes, over leaves, over windows and roads. As an icicle I stretch to the tallest, as a sheet to the thinnest, as a floe to the widest. As a glacier I grow heavy, squashing the land, gouging valleys out of mountains, ponds out of pinnacles. I seize, I freeze. That is my way.

I am snow. Part water, part crystal, part miniature star. Feather and diamond bonded as one. My life is a flight, twirling and gliding. Though I am distinct from all my trillions of cousins, we are so alike in our luminous hearts that we can coat canyons and cities and make them seem one. I whiten the land, brighten the air. I bring frosted galaxies down to the ground.

I am cloud. Rumbling, gathering, steaming, stretching. Vapors are my body, thin as a breath, yet thick enough to stop the sun. Finer than filigree, broader than basins. Cumulus, nimbus, cirrus and stratus. Whatever I yield shall float back to me. My gifts to the world are always returned.

I am ocean. Raging and bitter, glassy and great. I move with the moon, I ride with the tides. Smelling of brine, brimming with life, tasting like salty kelp stew. No roads cross my surface, no sun shines below. I am the edges of continents, the bottoms of chasms, the peaks of tsunamis. Though my waters lie deep, my mysteries lie deeper still.

And with time, Kate understood that she held within her all these forms. She could swim with the wave, sail with the mist. Her body wrapped around her like a flowing tail, transparent as dew and subtly gleaming. Liquid as the sea itself, she swept into the swirling vapors above the old ship, gracefully rising.

For now she was a water spirit.

Soon the mist deepened into fog, the fog into droplets, the

droplets into heaving waves. The current whirled her around, faster and faster. Immense waves pressed into her, flattening her to nothingness.

For an age she spun through these reeling waters. Then, gradually, the pressure reduced. Though she had no need to breathe, she felt her body expand, and she drank of the wide ocean again.

Darkness surrounded her, except for some strange and shadowy lights that circled and flickered. She could no longer see the ship. In every direction, deep currents throbbed, flowing into underwater canyons and around the roots of islands. She had passed through the whirlpool.

PART THREE:
BEYOND THE ABYSS

XXI
BATTLE IN THE DEPTHS

K ate soon discovered she could swim in an entirely new way, without stroking or kicking. Such motions were impossible anyway, since her new body, which had expanded in size once she emerged from the whirlpool, bore no arms and no legs. Something of a cross between a transparent jellyfish and a slender frond of kelp, she possessed a lithe, ribbonlike form. She was, in fact, little more than a long and lacy tail. She needed only to sway herself from side to side, undulating with the currents, to move in any direction, including up and down.

A group of thin fish swam past, their tails and jaws radiating blue phosphorescent light. Twisted black smokers jutted off the sea floor like shrunken volcanoes, venting bright clouds of chemicals that illuminated the water while making it taste of rotten eggs. Giant white clams, so large they made the Venus clams of the lagoon look like mere infants, clung to the base of the smoking vents. Kate flowed past one of them, feeling its intense heat. She knew that it spewed superheated gases, boiling bile from the center of the Earth.

As she swam, swaying gracefully, the humming of the whirlpool faded behind her. More strange life forms appeared on all sides. Tube worms, clustered together in bizarre bouquets, bent and curled in slow motion. Their tops opened in scarlet plumes, possibly a kind of mouth for drinking the chemicals billowing from the smokers. A ghostly crab bolted away as she approached, sliding into a narrow crevasse. Tiny blue limpets, oversized snails, and wormlike larvae congregated on the rocks.

Then, in the dim light, she perceived another shape. Huge, streamlined, and gray, it floated just above the bottom, completely motionless. It possessed an enormous tail, wider than she was long. Just behind its jaw, a great eye regarded her cautiously.

A whale.

Almost imperceptibly, she wafted nearer. The whale, an adult male, did not stir, following her movements with his unblinking eye. Before long, she could see the cluster of barnacles on his belly and tail, the knobs of his vertebrae, the twin blowholes.

Suddenly, the massive back arched and snapped, sending the whale gliding away into the shadowy depths. The current washed over Kate, rolling her backward. She brushed against a cluster of tube worms, felt them tickle the full length of her body.

As the whale departed, he began to whistle in a low, haunting voice. Soon other invisible singers joined him, wailing and weeping, reliving their sorrows. Kate listened quietly, feeling her own longings. Dad . . . a prisoner of Nimue. *I've got to find him.* But how? He could be anywhere.

At once she sensed that something apart from herself had frightened the whale. Curious, she whirled around.

Swimming awkwardly, a most unusual creature approached. Although shaped somewhat like herself, this figure looked spindly, even shriveled. It resembled more a twisted root than a graceful tail. Jerkily, it swam toward her, evidently eager to communicate.

The creature blinked its single swollen eye, the color of blue-tinted ice. Then it spoke to Kate telepathically, in a voice she recognized with a twinge.

"Where the devil are we?" asked Terry. "And *what* are we?"

"I was hoping you had stayed behind."

"So had I. Guess, ah, you were right about the book. You're full of surprises."

Kate felt a surge of both pleasure and embarrassment. In her old body, she would have blushed.

"So tell me. What are we?"

"We're some kind of water creatures, I guess." A laugh bubbled up. "You look a little on the skinny side, though."

"Incredible," said Terry, curling his transparent tail so he could see it. "I still can't believe this is real."

"As real as the ship and the whirlpool." She spun slowly in the water. "Why did you decide to follow me?"

"I didn't. I just found myself here." The bulbous eye blinked. "How do we get our old bodies back?"

"Maybe Geoffrey can do that, if we ever find him again." She resumed swimming. "That won't be easy, though. He had a good head start. You can bet he's on his way to the Glass House, wherever that is."

Struggling to stay with her, Terry called, "Listen, are you crazy? We've got to get out of here before the eruption happens. As far away as possible, while we still have time."

"You do what you want," she replied, waving her tail more rapidly. "But I'm going to try to find my dad, if I can."

Terry hesitated, then tried to keep pace with her. "You're

not getting rid of me that easily," he grumbled. "I'll stay with you, at least until we can figure out how to get our old bodies back. Hey, what's that?"

Both of them stopped short, staring at the cloud pouring from a smoker straight ahead. They watched the cloud slowly rising into the water, pulsing with reddish light.

"Did you see that?"

"I'm not sure," she replied. "It was there, beside that cloud. Then it vanished."

"It looked like something out of a fable," he said, a touch of awe in his voice.

Kate, studying the smoking vent, did not answer for some time. "It could have been the weird light down here, playing tricks."

"Could have been. But I'm sure I saw it. And it looked just like . . ." He paused, unable to say the word. "Like a *mermaid.*"

Together they floated, silently waiting, hoping to glimpse it again. But they saw nothing beyond the glowing fumes.

"Let's go," said Kate at last. She slid through the water, waving her gossamery form. Despite her fears, she still could not help but enjoy the feeling of weightlessness, of being so insubstantial that she was almost part of the water itself. Then, with a sharp pang, she thought of her father and Isabella. Even if she could possibly find them, would it be in time? And what could she hope to do to help them? Seeing a house-size boulder covered with a thick mat of yellow vegetation, she drifted toward it, occupied with her thoughts.

At once, the boulder stirred. From under its hulking form, more than a dozen burly legs extended, groping on the rocks. The vegetation, so soft and swaying from a distance, hardened into murderous spikes, each one as long as a lance. The monster, with narrow slits where eyes might once have been, lifted itself from its lair and opened its gargantuan mouth, where an army of tongues rippled like a nest of blood red worms.

"Look out!"

The pair turned and whipped through the water. But the spidery creature pursued them relentlessly, crashing over fuming vents and rock outcroppings. The faster they swam, the nearer it drew, legs churning, snarling angrily. Beads of brown sludge oozed from the edges of its mouth.

Glancing to the rear, Kate could see the monster pulling nearer. Terry, swimming clumsily, had fallen so far behind her that the beast was almost on top of him.

"Hellllp!" he cried. "It's going to—"

As his words disappeared in an avalanche of snarling, Kate spotted a shallow cave about equidistant between them. Without thinking, she reversed her direction and raced back toward it, throwing herself directly into Terry and driving them both into the mouth of the cave. They wriggled inside just as the monster arrived.

Protected by a ledge of overhanging rock, they pressed against the back of the cave. The cries of the creature echoed around them, rising in repeating crescendos. Then, inexplicably, the noise ceased.

For several minutes they waited, not daring to move. Still as stone, they could only hope that the monster had finally given up and departed.

"There!" screamed Kate.

A long, leathery leg reached into the cave, slithering toward them. They shrank still deeper into their burrow, even as the leg lashed out at them. It grazed Kate's flank, but could not quite reach her.

For an instant the leg seemed to hesitate. Then it planted itself against the rock ledge directly above them. The snarling resumed, as the leg began pulling on the roof of the cave, trying to tear it away.

A jagged piece of rock broke loose. Kate grabbed it in the folds of her tail and stabbed at the leg. The creature roared wrathfully, but kept its leg in place. Harder and harder it pulled. The water in the cave grew murky with crumbling rock.

All at once, the rock ledge buckled. Before Kate or Terry knew what had happened, the slab flew off, exposing the cave. There, gaping at them, was the cavernous mouth. The squirming tongues stretched toward them.

Then, in a shriek of pain, the monster jerked backward. A titanic tail wrapped around its body, squeezing mercilessly. The yellow spikes snapped off like stalactites as the beast writhed and kicked, trying to free itself from its attacker, a great blue scorpion with a poisonous barb and slashing fangs.

Great clouds of sediment rose all around as the two leviathans wrestled, battling in the depths. The scorpion's fangs ripped at the flesh of its opponent, even as powerful legs tried to break its back. On and on they fought, screaming and roaring, pounding themselves against the sea floor.

Kate and Terry could do no more than cower in the small hollow that once had been a cave. They waited for some chance to escape, knowing it would probably never come. Meanwhile, the battle grew ever more violent. The monsters thrashed and tumbled, battering each other's bodies, unwilling to stop until one lay vanquished.

Finally, the legs of the spiderlike beast hung limp. The blue scorpion lifted its head and bellowed a cry of victory.

"Don't move," whispered Kate. "Maybe it will go away."

"Don't bet on it," Terry replied nervously.

Using its great barb, the scorpion butted the corpse fiercely, making sure its adversary would not rise and strike again. Finally, coiling its tail, it seemed to prepare to crawl away, when suddenly it halted. Spotting the two gleaming forms in the hollow, it stretched its neck toward them.

The colossal head lowered until it hung only a few feet above Kate and Terry. Darkly, the scorpion's indigo eyes examined them. Then it opened its jaws, baring the horrible fangs.

XXII

THE PASSAGE

As the deadly fangs draped over them, the two water spirits huddled tightly together.

"You shouldn't have come back for me," grumbled Terry. "That was stupid."

"Guess so," Kate said sullenly.

"I suppose I should say thanks."

"I suppose I should say you're welcome."

Just then, something odd happened. The fangs began to melt into seawater, along with the rest of the scorpion's head. The blue armor covering the length of its body grew steadily lighter in color, fading to the point of transparency. The indigo eyes flashed for the last time. Then, with a slight *pop*, the scorpion disappeared completely.

Floating in its place, barely as large as one of the fangs, was a grotesque little fish with a beaklike nose. The entire body was covered with scraggly white hairs, while the dorsal fin wriggled energetically, as if trying to scratch. Then, to the astonishment of Kate and Terry, the fish spoke.

"I never should have shown you the book."

"Geoffrey!" whooped Kate. "It's you."

The fish opened his jaws to the widest, much as the scorpion had done, then gurgled noisily before snapping them shut. "Pardon my yawning," he said grumpily. Swimming closer to Terry, the fish eyed him suspiciously. "And what, may I ask, is this?"

"The same could be asked of you," answered Terry. "I never thought I'd owe my life to a scrawny old fish."

"Delighted to be of service," came the reply. "Actually, before you arrived I was searching for some way to slip past the many-legged creature." His thin mouth pinched as he fought to hold back a yawn. "Thanks to you, I was able to mount a surprise attack."

"Where," asked Kate as quietly as she could, "is the Horn?"

The fish looked at her slyly, then uncurled a small fin under his tail just enough to reveal a gleaming object tucked inside. "Reduced in size, but safe enough." The fin closed tight again. "Well now, if you're going to accompany me—"

"Yes!" exclaimed Kate, her whole transparent body vibrating. Then she fell still. "Was that creature you killed related to the spider monster who guarded the entrance to the land of Shaa?"

The old fish blew a bubble, which expanded to the size of his head before popping. "No doubt."

"Does that mean the entrance to Shaa is near?"

"Nearer than you know." The fish's white mane quivered. "The land of Shaa lies at the bottom of a great abyss. *Darkest of the dark*, as it is known in legend."

"That's the only way I want to know it," said Kate.

"You may not wish to accompany me, then."

"You mean—?"

His dorsal fin wriggling, the old fish said grimly, "That is the way, the only way, to the Glass House. For the Glass House and the land of Shaa lie on the same path. If you are going to join me, you must travel down the same dark passage as Emrys and Merlin did long ago."

Kate felt suddenly limp.

"You can go back to the ship in the way you came, if you choose. I shall do my best to send word."

Her single-celled form tensed. "I'm coming with you."

The old fish studied her. "Are you quite sure?"

"Quite sure."

"Well then, as I was saying, if you're going to accompany me, you will need to dress more appropriately. A disguise, what? As you are, you'll soon end up as salad for one of Nimue's sea demons."

Terry swung his silver-blue eye toward the monstrous corpse, whose mouth gaped wide, its tongues hanging limp. "Whatever sea demons are, they can't be as bad as that thing over there."

Shaking himself, the old fish said to Kate, "He doesn't know very much, does he?"

"No," she replied. "But he's learning."

"Don't count on it." Terry turned to Geoffrey. "I won't delay you any longer. Would you mind changing me so I can get out of here?"

"It will be a pleasure," replied the fish. He burbled some syllables and waved his fin awkwardly.

Pop. Terry's watery shape vanished. In its place swam an ugly fish with goggle eyes, the same kind of fish that Isabella had analyzed in her makeshift laboratory.

"Hey, what's going on?" sputtered Terry. "I meant change me into a person. Not a fish version of Frankenstein! Change me back. Right now!"

"That might be risky," answered Geoffrey. "In the first place, people don't survive very long at the bottom of the sea. In the second place, I am not sure I can do it. Going from human to animal is much easier than the other way around. You might end up as a peacock or a giraffe."

Kate could not suppress a giggle. "That might be an improvement."

Pop. She found herself as an elegant fish with emerald green scales and a phosphorescent stripe down both sides. Elegant, but for the fact that in her nose she sported a large brass ring.

"What's this?" she exclaimed. "There's a ring in my nose."

"A nice touch," pronounced Terry.

"My apologies," said Geoffrey. "It's happened to me before. I must work on that charm."

"Can't you make it disappear?"

"Unfortunately not," he sighed. "A quirky business, this. At least I got the luminous stripes right. You can be our torch. There is no light where we are going."

With a quick jackknife he darted away, followed a few seconds later by Kate and Terry, muttering to themselves about their new forms. The white-haired fish led them across the ocean floor, offering a running commentary about how to swim like a fish.

"Your head is sagging," coached Geoffrey. "Look dead ahead."

"Easy for you to say," huffed Kate. "I've got this stupid ring in my nose."

She tried again.

"Not like that! You're weaving like a drunkard. Use your spine. Your whole spine."

"Here, I'll show you," offered Terry. "It's easy once you

get the hang of it." He gave a sharp jerk of his tail and promptly flipped over backward.

"Gee, thanks," moaned Kate.

After several false starts, however, she started to move with some confidence. Before long she and the others reached the very spot where they had encountered the spidery creature. As they approached, a black chasm loomed before them. Wider than a whale, it looked impossibly deep and utterly dark, illuminated only by the faint glow of a smoking vent nearby.

"Is that it?" asked Kate doubtfully.

Geoffrey eyed the chasm. "The abyss."

"You're joking," said Terry as he cautiously approached the edge. "Magma is pushing higher all the time! Going down there would be like swimming straight into the eruption."

"You can wait for us here if you prefer," offered Geoffrey, circling slowly above the entrance. "Of course, you might have to deal with the mother of your many-legged friend. And she might not be in a very jolly mood when she returns."

With that, Geoffrey dived into the abyss. Not far behind came Kate, whose phosphorescent stripes cast a pale blue light on the jagged rock walls, and behind her, a reluctant Terry.

Suddenly, a fissure opened in the rock just ahead of them. Molten lava bubbled out, sizzling like hot coals doused with water. The walls of the abyss trembled as the space filled with a distant rumbling. Gradually, the fiery lava dimmed, hardening into stone before their eyes.

"As if it weren't hot enough in here already," said Geoffrey, jackknifing past the fissure.

"This is insane," objected Terry, starting to retreat.

Kate beckoned to him with her fin.

"But we'll be fried fish fillets if we go any deeper."

"It's our only chance," she replied, darting past the smoldering stone. She did not look back, but waited to hear him swim again before she continued.

Downward they swam, plunging into the chasm. Despite the uncomfortable warmth of the water, Kate felt increasingly gripped by a strange chill, a chill she had felt somewhere before. The vague, half-formed memory of a nightmare swelled inside her. It was not a matter of temperature, or of anything physical. Something about this place blew biting cold on her innermost self. The chill only deepened as they descended.

"Douse the torch!" ordered Geoffrey.

Kate obeyed. The abyss fell raven black. Although she could not see, she still could feel. The icy feeling grew stronger, working into her bones, her brain, her blood. *Darkest of the dark*. She wanted to shriek. At that instant a shadowed figure swept by, rising out of the depths. It brushed her with its frozen breath as it passed.

In time, she dared speak again. "What was that?"

"I don't want to know," said Terry, shaken.

"A sea demon." Geoffrey's tail twitched nervously. "We must be doubly careful now. We should proceed without any light."

Terry frowned. "But I can't do that. I'll swim straight into a wall."

"Not advisable," the elder fish replied crisply. "Stay right with me, close as you can."

Following his suggestion, Kate positioned herself immediately behind Geoffrey, while Terry trailed her closely. Sometimes, especially rounding bends, they would bump into one another, jamming faces into tails. As they continued, though, they swam with increasing coordination. Kate gradually became aware of a new sense guiding her motions, that ancient instinct that binds a school of fish together as they swim in unison. In time their three bodies moved almost as one.

For what might have been hours they voyaged downward. At last, ever so slowly, Kate discerned a subtle light ahead. For a while she thought it was merely her own wishful thinking. Yet the passage was indeed growing less dark. The abyss began to widen and to dive less steeply, even as it brightened. Finally they entered a great cavern, wider and taller than they could tell.

Geoffrey angled upward, leading the others. With a trio of splashes, they broke through the surface of what appeared to be a lake, set inside the expansive cavern.

"Air," puzzled Kate, keeping her gills underwater. "How did air get down here?"

"The sea holds many surprises," answered Geoffrey. He swished his tail, then said, "If you look up, you will see another."

XXIII
SEA STARS

Raising her eyes to the ceiling of the cavern, Kate saw the one thing she least expected to find, far beneath the stormy surface of the ocean.

Stars. Hundreds of them, thousands of them. Shimmering with an eerie undersea light, beaming down upon the little band. Like an endless procession of candles, the stars vaulted overhead, illuminating the immense chamber.

She could see none of the familiar constellations she had come to know during her evenings at the research station, when the dome of night had risen over San Lazaro Lagoon. Yet here she found a myriad of new patterns and shapes, clusters and swirls. Galaxies upon galaxies adorned the cavern, floating in fairylike reflection on the water. And, as ever, the spaces between the stars spoke to her of wonder and infinity.

Then a familiar wailing echoed, a song of loss and longing. The three companions listened in silence.

Geoffrey swayed his dorsal fin. "Whales may wander far and wide, seeking some way to ease their pain, but it does them no good. Even such a flowering of undersea stars cannot soothe them."

"I remember," said Kate wistfully, "my dad's stories about Merlin."

Geoffrey's fin stopped moving. "Yes?"

"He told me how sometimes Merlin would enter a cave, someplace blacker than night, and take off his cape that was studded with stars. Then he would flick his cape in such a way that the stars would float up and stick to the ceiling of the cave. So when anyone else came, it would be light instead of dark. My dad said that if you ever found a cave like that, you could tell that Merlin had been there."

"Hmmmm," said Geoffrey. "I rather like that story. Perhaps it is true."

"And perhaps it is just a story," replied Terry.

Geoffrey examined him with reptile eyes. "So you don't believe in Merlin?"

"Believe he really existed? No, I'm afraid not. He makes a fine legend, I'll give you that much. I don't expect to run into him on the street, though."

"You might run into someone who knew him," cautioned Geoffrey.

"Meaning Nimue?" asked Kate.

The white mane bristled. "Do not speak that name. We are close. Too close."

At that moment a fragrant wind, full of the smells of the sea, swept over them. Kate suddenly noticed that, on every wall of the cavern, waterfalls gathered and tumbled into the lake. The water within them sparkled with such purity that the cascades seemed to glow with liquid light.

Here we are, she thought, in the realm of Shaa. *The place where the sea begins, the womb where the waters are born.* Then, in a hushed voice, she asked, "Where is the castle of Merwas?"

Geoffrey simply plunged downward, leaving her question unanswered.

They swam just deep enough in the warm currents to coast along the border between light and dark. Below, all was black. Above, the horizon stretched over them like a shining circle, perfectly round. Within this circle danced the stars, seeming to belong first to water and only second to air.

Once Kate glimpsed a solitary form swimming above them. Its shape was blurred, but it appeared to possess the tail of a fish and the upper body of a man. She turned to Geoffrey to catch his attention, but by the time she looked back, it had disappeared.

Before long, the lake began to smell richer, like the scent of deep woods in autumn. A few trunks of kelp rose from the bottom, with fronds so intricate and plentiful that Kate had to swim carefully to avoid entangling her brass ring. Prickly sea urchins clung to rocks. Eels drifted lazily past.

Fish of all sorts wove their ways through the sparkling water. Some, as slim as snakes, encircled the swaying trunks of kelp that climbed upward from the bottom. Others, brightly painted, inhabited the colonies of pink and purple coral shaped like lacy fans, bulbous horns, or grooved brains. Passing nearby, Kate could hear hungry fish biting the corals with their teeth, crunching and scraping in search of food. Towering sponges, splashed with colors, sprouted on all sides. And from dens under ledges, shadowed eyes watched with interest.

Surrounded by the jungle of coral and its many inhabitants, Geoffrey slowed his pace. He swam almost leisurely, hardly bending his back. At length, he surfaced again. The others followed.

Kate gasped. Facing them stood a glorious castle with walls made of streaming, spraying waterfalls. Thundering and crashing, it lifted high out of the lake, glittering in the starlight, a tower of sculpted water. Columns of cascading liquid supported its turrets and buttresses. Archways made of rainbows ran along the rims of its battlements. Stairs of lavender coral spiraled into its rampways and towers, leading to halls and chambers hidden behind crystalline curtains.

"The Glass House," she said in wonderment.

"Known in other times," added Geoffrey, "as the castle of Merwas."

Kate fluttered her fins. "So they are the same!"

"One and the same."

Viewing the magnificent castle, she said, "What a place to hide the Treasures."

"Yes," agreed the white-haired fish. "It made good sense at the time. Remember that when Merlin found his way here, the entire realm of Shaa, including this castle, was deserted. Not only had the mer people fled, but . . . the sorceress, having searched fruitlessly for the Horn, had abandoned the cavern as well. And so Merlin believed," Geoffrey added dismally, "that it would stay that way. He simply did not count on the fact that one day she would return here and discover the hidden Treasures. Or that she would willingly destroy the Glass House and everything in it, not to mention the whirlpool and the ship and much else besides, just to get the Horn."

"That N—"

"Hush!" commanded Geoffrey, looking around fearfully.

"Sorry," she replied. "I won't slip again. I promise."

Focusing again on the Glass House, she followed the contours of its flowing walls. Then she gasped again. For at the base of one of the battlements, partially concealed by a fountain, she spied a large silver shape. *The submersible.*

She had no chance to cry out. In an instant, the castle vanished and the stars eclipsed. The world went dark, dark as the abyss.

XXIV

PRISONERS

Kate awoke, shivering. *The water here is so cold I feel numb.* She reached to rub her sore head. Reached, she realized all of a sudden, with her own hand.

She sat bolt upright. Though this place was very dark, she could still make out the shape of her hand. She closed it into a fist, then reopened it. She touched her face, her hair, her arms. *No more brass ring.* She took a deep breath. *No more gills.* Her head still throbbed. All she could see in the dim light was water, running and rushing from all directions. And all she could feel was wet and cold.

A strong hand reached out of the shadows and clasped her by the forearm.

"Terry?"

"Glad you're back with the living. I was getting worried there." Glancing over his shoulder, he said, "Especially when old Geoffrey had you looking like a partridge."

"An unavoidable detour," grumbled the old man, emerging from the shadows. He scratched the tip of his pointed nose. "I had to do it to get rid of the ring."

"That's not what you said when it happened," Terry reminded him. "But you got it right in the end, as you did with me."

"You mean to tell me," queried Geoffrey innocently, "you didn't like being a donkey?"

"Not in the least."

"Once an ass, always an ass."

"All right, you two," interjected Kate, clambering to her feet. She sloshed a few steps across the wet floor. "Where are we, anyway?"

"We are in the dungeon." Geoffrey's morose face came closer. "Somewhere under the Glass House."

"The dungeon! How did we get here?"

"We were captured. By the sea demons. For some reason they didn't kill us on the spot, but merely rendered us senseless and threw us in here."

"Have you looked around for a way to escape?"

Geoffrey eyed her somberly. "Since regaining our human forms, that is *all* we have been doing. But although these walls and this floor are made only of water, they are as sturdy as iron."

"Dad and Isabella are somewhere around here, too! I saw the submersible."

"Yes," answered the monk. "Though I cannot tell you where they might be, or in what condition."

"We have to find them." She flapped her arms to warm herself. "Why is it so c-cold in here? It's been getting hotter and hotter as the eruption gets nearer. But now I'm f-f-freezing."

"I will show you," answered Geoffrey. He led her over to a squarish hole in the wall where no water flowed.

"A window," she marveled, shivering again.

"Come nearer. You can see the lake. And something more."

"Are you sure she's strong enough?" asked Terry.

"I'm f-fine," said Kate, not really feeling that way. She approached the window, peering out at the starlit cavern and the still water below. "It's darker in here than out there," she observed.

Geoffrey nodded. "These walls—see how thick they are?—keep out much of the light from the stars. And Nimue has not equipped her dungeon with a torch."

"You never answered my question. About the c-cold."

"The truth is," Geoffrey explained, "it is quite warm in here."

"But I feel—"

"You feel cold. You feel chilled to the bone. That is because you were touched."

"Touched? By what?"

Geoffrey raised his arm and pointed his knobby finger out the window. "By one of them."

Kate turned again to the glistening surface of the lake, just as a whitecap appeared. From beneath it came a dark form, rising slowly to the surface. At first she thought it was an enormous eel, but the intense chill in her chest told her otherwise. She watched, transfixed, as it lifted its huge, triangular head above the water.

The sea demon spun a half rotation, growled fiercely, then fell back with a colossal splash. In two seconds it was gone, yet that was all she needed to view the massive body covered with purple scales, the savage jaw, the teeth sharp as knives. The sight seemed to fill her whole body with ice.

Then a hand, larger than hers, slid into her own. It was Terry, standing beside her. As she turned to him in thanks, the chill seemed to lessen a bit. Little by little, she felt her lungs breathing and her heart pumping, with growing strength and growing warmth.

"Do you think," she asked quietly, "we still have a chance? If not to stop Nimue, at least to save Dad and Isabella?"

Terry stroked the cleft of his chin. "That depends on how soon the eruption hits. With these tremors and vents bursting open . . . my guess is we have only a few minutes left, at the most." He observed her thoughtfully. "But whatever we have, I suppose it's something."

Lightly, she squeezed his hand.

Geoffrey approached, the breeze from the window ruffling his unruly hair. "It is a bleak moment," he confessed. "Bleaker because I must share it with both of you."

"We came by our own choice," said Kate.

"By your own folly," corrected Geoffrey. "And by my folly as well. I fear we have arrived too late to stop Nimue from destroying everything. And even if we did have enough time, what could we do?" He shrugged disspiritedly. "The days of the Glass House, and Arthur's final hope, are ended."

"You don't know that yet," insisted Kate.

The old man locked into her gaze. Somewhere behind his eyes, a frail fire kindled. "Perhaps." He patted the folds of cloth over his chest where the last of the Treasures lay hidden. "You remind me that we still possess the one thing Nimue most craves. And she will not get it easily."

"Couldn't we take a drink from the Horn? Maybe its power could help us."

Geoffrey shook his head. "Whatever the Horn's power truly is, no one who has not first met the test of the Emperor Merwas may drink from it. Merlin learned that painful lesson! In any case, I doubt that taking a drink would help us stop Nimue. The Horn's power is of a . . . different nature." He scratched behind his neck. "Yet you do make me wonder. Perhaps—"

At that moment, a blinding light flashed. When Kate's vision cleared, she could see that a door had opened in the liquid wall of the dungeon.

"Oh no," she said.

"Good Lord," muttered Geoffrey, placing his hand over his chest.

XXV
FIRST LOYALTY

Astout, square-shouldered man stood in the doorway,
sizing up the group. In one burly hand he held a torch, but its
light burned dimly compared to the glowing sword he held in
the other. His face looked weathered and wrinkled, though
less from outer storms than from inner ones. A torn oilskin
shirt hung over his chest, the sleeves long ago removed. The
hair on his head, blond and curly, matched that sprouting
from his close-cropped beard as well as his biceps. His nose
was swollen and inflamed, but the rest of his skin was white,
like someone who has not seen the sun for many years.

Kate glanced at Geoffrey. He could not take his eyes off
the shining sword of light. For her, however, it was the man's
eyes that caught her curiosity. They were dark as night,
much like the monk's, but with a difference. While Geoffrey's eyes seemed younger than the rest of him, this man's
eyes seemed considerably older, as if his body had remained
frozen in time while his eyes had continued to age.

"Welcome to my castle," he declared with a rolling accent
that was made more pronounced by his stuffy nose.

Geoffrey started to speak, caught himself, then stuffed the end of his beard into his mouth and chewed vigorously.

"I am Garl-a-a-ah-ah-*choooo!*" He unceremoniously wiped his nose on his shirt, then cursed, "Damn this cold." With a loud sniff, he began again. "I am Garlon the Seaworthy, master of this house."

Geoffrey chewed still harder.

"I should have sent my servants to fetch you, but they are, ah, busy just now."

Apparently no longer able to stand it, Geoffrey tore the beard from his mouth and said, "If you mean Nimue and her sea demons, it is they who are the masters and you who are the servant."

Flame kindled in Garlon's eyes, and he raised the brilliant sword. "Who are you, who dares to speak to me this way?"

"I am Geoffrey of Bardsey, of the Order of the Horn."

Garlon pounced to Geoffrey's side. Thrusting the blade at the old man's throat, he said, "Geoffrey of Bardsey. Ah, yes. I understand you have a little a-a-ah-*choo!* . . . a little something I have long awaited."

Geoffrey tried to back away, but found himself pressed against a coursing wall of water.

"Leave him alone," shouted Kate. "Can't you see he has no weapons?"

Garlon whirled around. "His sharp tongue is weapon enough! He is nothing but a slimy old bag of bones, better off dead."

"Now, now," said Geoffrey, his eyes focused on the point of the sword and his whole body quivering, "I really didn't mean to offend you."

Garlon wiped his nose again. "Then why did you insult me?"

Still staring at the sword, Geoffrey laughed nervously. "I didn't think you would take it so personally."

Garlon jabbed the sword closer to his throat.

"It was just a spot of humor," said Geoffrey, squirming at the sword point.

"Well, I have no time for humor." He jerked the weapon away from Geoffrey, who nearly collapsed with relief. "I should kill you now, but Nimue wants to do it herself." Waving the sword toward the door, he commanded with the authority of a sea captain, "Go now. The whole crew of you."

Terry led the way out of the dungeon, stumbling in the dim light. He was followed by Kate and, last of all, Geoffrey. Garlon, torch held high, marched them down a hallway and up a long, spiraling staircase of lavender coral. The stairs seemed to twirl upward without end, climbing inside a curtain of crashing water. Geoffrey, tiring, dragged himself more and more slowly. Occasionally, Garlon prodded him with the sharp tip of the radiant sword.

At last the stairway peaked, opening into a room as spacious as any Kate had ever seen. On every side, powerful fountains formed rows of arches, one flowing into the next. The walls of water splashed and bubbled ceaselessly. Overhead, gushing jets of water merged into a vaulted ceiling.

"The great hall," panted Geoffrey, looking exhausted but awestruck.

Kate nodded, but her attention was directed not to the vast room, drained of water as Merlin had found it long ago. Nor was it directed to the array of objects near the glistening throne in the center of the floor. Instead she felt drawn to a large cage at the far edge of the great hall. Within its liquid bars, dark shapes moved.

"Dad!" she cried, running to the cage.

"Kate! Is that you?"

"It's me!" She sprinted past the empty throne. "Are you all right?"

"A little wet, but yes," her father replied.

"A lot wet." Isabella shook herself. "But at least we are alive, eh?"

"I'm so glad. I thought maybe . . ." Tears brimming, Kate held his hand through the watery bars. It felt strong. And alive. And Dad. "We've got to get you out of here."

"I've tried," he answered. "Believe me, I have. It's impossible. Until that sorceress comes back."

"Nimue," said Kate bitterly. She could almost picture the enchantress, her smoky body, her bottomless eyes . . . almost as if she had seen her somewhere before. But of course she had not. Kate released her father's grip and shook the bars with rage. "She's going to wipe out this whole place, and all of us, just to get—"

"The Horn," completed Garlon, standing behind her. He sneezed, spraying all of them. "That's right. Only Nimue and I can let them out. And she ordered—er, asked—me not to do that."

Jim wiped his face on his sleeve and shook his head in disgust. "Remind me, if I ever get out of this, to revise the accounts of Garlon the brave and heroic seaman." Then, spying Terry and Geoffrey across the room, he asked, "Is that Terry? And who is with him?"

"Yes, Terry," answered Kate, watching him help the old man hobble slowly toward them. "He's not so bad, you know. And that's Geoffrey. He's a monk. We found him on the *Resurrección*."

"The *Resurrección!*" exclaimed her father. "You've *been* there?"

Kate nodded.

"And the old man was there?"

"Went down with the ship. He stayed alive thanks to—" She caught herself, seeing Garlon listening closely. "I'll tell you later."

Her father reached his hand out of the cage and brushed her braid. "As much as I wanted to see you again, I had hoped it wouldn't be here."

She bit her lip.

"And as much as I dreamed of one day seeing the Treasures," he went on, "I never thought I'd see them through the bars of a cage."

"They're about to be destroyed, if Nimue has her way."

"I know. She thinks that she can cause some kind of disturbance—an earthquake or something—that will wreck the Glass House, as well as the whirlpool. She was boasting, just before you came, that when the whirlpool collapses, she can make off with the Horn. Unless of course, as she put it, she can lure someone into bringing her the Horn first."

Kate winced, then turned to the throne, which seemed to be made of millions of crystalline water droplets. *The throne of Merwas.* And surrounding it, the Treasures. Placed on one of its wide arms was the chessboard, with several wooden pieces sitting on it, awaiting someone's next move. Some distance away sat the flaming chariot, burning with such intense heat that it made the castle floor steam around its base.

Nearby, many other legendary objects were gathered. She spotted the knife, the pan, and the whetstone, all resting on top of a glassy table. The mantle of invisibility, copper-red in hue, leaned against a towering column of water, along with the halter and the harp. On the floor by the throne sat the ever-bubbling cauldron of knowledge, black, wide-mouthed, and nearly as tall as Kate herself. At its base lay the vessel of plenty, spilling forth a feast of fruits, cheeses, and dried venison, plus a large goblet of red wine.

The Treasures of the Isle of Britain. They represented all that humankind might need to live comfortably, and all that Arthur might need to triumph in his final battle.

She counted them. Ten were by the throne. The sword of light made eleven. The Horn was twelve. What was missing? Oh, yes—the ring. Now what was it that happened to the ring? Somehow she could not remember.

Just then Geoffrey and Terry veered off course and headed straight for the vessel of plenty. Garlon, seeing this, ran to intercept them. He leaped in front of them just as Geoffrey bent toward the goblet of wine.

"Just hoping for a swallow or two," grumbled the old man, eyeing the goblet.

"No," ordered Garlon. "I a-a-ah-*choooo!*" He wiped his nose. "I will tell you what you can touch and what you cannot."

"You know," said Geoffrey innocently, "that cold sounds positively *abysmal.* No humor intended, you understand. I know just the thing to cure it."

Garlon's eyebrows raised. "What?"

"What you need," explained Geoffrey with the barest hint of a smirk, "is a good dose of sunshine."

"Impudent swine!" fumed Garlon. He started to rush at Geoffrey, then held himself back. "I will kill you later," he promised. "After Nimue is done with you." A slow smile spread over his face. "And then I will drink from the Horn."

Kate drew near. "Do you really think Nimue will let you do that?"

"Who are you, girl?" demanded Garlon. "Tell me your name."

"Kate Gordon."

"A girl," said Garlon contemptuously. "And do you also belong to the Order of the Horn?"

"No," she replied. Then, with a glance at Geoffrey, she added, "But I'd like to."

Garlon laughed raucously, then rubbed his tender nose. "So that is the best the enemies of Garlon and Nimue can do? To send an old man and a girl?" Again he laughed, pointing the torch at Terry. "And a coward."

Terry stepped forward in a huff, but Geoffrey grabbed his shirt.

"Careful," whispered the old man. "The sword of light can cut you to pieces in the blink of an eye."

"Don't you see what you're doing?" pleaded Kate. "You're going to ruin all of Merlin's work."

Garlon scowled. "Merlin. Bah! Don't speak that name! I am only sorry he is already dead, so I cannot kill him myself." He threw the torch at the flaming chariot, which instantly consumed it. "My gift to Merlin is to destroy the Glass House. Forever!"

Geoffrey scratched behind his neck. "Now I understand. Nimue must have tapped the power of the chariot to make the rocks under the sea seethe with fire until they erupt."

Garlon started to nod before stopping to contain a sneeze.

"I don't believe it," sneered Terry. "How can some chariot cause a volcanic eruption?"

"What are you, an alchemist?" shot back Garlon. "I will show you what the chariot can do." He planted both feet firmly, then pointed his sword at the flaming vehicle.

"No!" cried Geoffrey.

At once, the flames leaped higher, almost to the ceiling of the great hall. From the chariot came a blast of heat like a mammoth furnace, so strong it knocked Geoffrey over back-

ward and made the others stagger, hands over their faces. A
distant roar gathered, swelling in volume until it drowned out
the cascading walls of the castle. Then the Glass House itself
shook, swaying violently from side to side, throwing Kate
and Terry to the floor.

Satisfied, Garlon lowered the luminous sword. The flames
fell back to their previous level, and the castle walls stopped
swaying. Surveying his prisoners as they scrambled to regain
their feet, he grunted in satisfaction.

Geoffrey leaned toward Terry and asked, "Do you believe
it now?"

He did not answer, but glared at Garlon.

As Kate stood, something fell out of her pocket and
slapped the floor. It was the ivory comb she had found near
the *Resurrección.*

She reached down and closed her hand around it. Suddenly Garlon barked, "What is that?"

"It's just a . . ." Kate's words trailed off as she felt herself
gripped by an idea. A desperate, wild idea.

"It's nothing," she said, cramming the comb back in her
pocket. "Nothing at all."

"Let me see it," he commanded.

"No."

Garlon lifted the sword again. "Let me see it."

She glanced at Geoffrey, still struggling to stand, and
Terry, who was trying to help him, then over her shoulder at
the cage holding her father and Isabella. Reluctantly, she
removed the lustrous comb from her pocket.

"You can't have it," she declared.

"I will decide that," retorted the seaman, grabbing it from
her. He held it before his face. "What is so special about a
comb?"

For an instant, Kate hesitated. She cleared her throat, as if she were about to reveal a precious secret. Then she announced, her voice full of drama, "You are holding . . . the greatest of all the Treasures. The Comb of Power."

Garlon cocked his head. "Go on."

"Didn't Nimue ever tell you about it? This is the one Treasure that has more power than all the others combined."

Garlon looked doubtful. "More than the Horn?"

"Much more."

He moved closer. "How does it work?"

"I will tell you," she promised. "But first you must agree to free the people in the cage."

"I could just kill you and keep it."

"If you kill me you'll never find out how to use it."

Garlon lowered his voice. "Would this make me more powerful than . . . *her*?"

She nodded. "You could tell her what to do for a change."

Still doubtful, he eyed Kate uncertainly. "Tell me how it works."

"First let them out of the cage. Before Nimue comes back."

Clutching the comb, Garlon debated what to do. He rubbed his nose distractedly.

Just then Geoffrey, who had finally righted himself, rushed over to his side. "You found it!" crowed the monk. "My missing comb! How good of you."

Garlon's nostrils flared. "Your comb?"

Oblivious to Kate's stricken look, Geoffrey went on, "This is number thirty-one thousand, eight hundred and forty-three."

"Treachery!" roared Garlon. Grabbing Kate by the shoulder, he shook her wrathfully. "It will be a pleasure to kill you." He raised the gleaming sword.

"Don't," cried Geoffrey, stepping between them.

"Get away, old man."

Geoffrey drew himself up, a mixture of scorn and pity in his eyes. "So is this what has become of Garlon the Sea-worthy? Reduced to striking down an unarmed girl?"

Garlon faltered, then snarled, "Whatever I am is because of Nimue. And that miserable Merlin."

"Merlin had nothing to do with your troubles! And if you hadn't listened to Nimue in the first place, you would never have been cursed by her."

"Bah! You are wrong."

"Even after what you did, Merlin might have found it in his heart to forgive you, from the depths of his tomb."

"You lie. Merlin hated me as much as I hated him."

"Ignored you, perhaps. But never hated you. If Merlin cast you aside, that was only because he was consumed with his desire to help Arthur."

A strange, smoldering fire shone in Garlon's eyes. "So you are saying that Merlin cared more for Arthur than he cared for his own brother?"

"Yes," answered Geoffrey. "You may have been Merlin's brother, but his first loyalty was to his king."

"Merlin's *brother*?" exclaimed Kate.

"It is true," Geoffrey went on. "Garlon is the lost brother of Merlin. Lost, in more ways than one."

"Enough of this." Garlon aimed his sword at Geoffrey's throat. "I am tired of waiting for Nimue. You will give me the Horn. Now!"

"No," hissed a voice behind him. "That will not be ne-cessssary."

XXVI
OLDEST AT BIRTH

Kate reeled with a rush of cold that clutched at her spine and clawed at her brain. Even the sweetness of apple blossoms in the air could not lessen her revulsion when she turned to see the sorceress.

Nimue stretched her gaseous arms toward Kate, twisting them like tentacles. Then she cocked her head, the only solid part of her form, and fluttered a misty finger. "You shall remember."

Suddenly their meeting came back to Kate. She remembered the blackened eyes, the steamlike voice—and the terrible bargain she had made to protect the life of her father. She knew that Nimue would not easily free her from whatever form of servitude she had in mind. And though Kate could not tell what that might be, the prospect filled her with dread.

"Sssso we meet again." Slowly, Nimue coiled her vaporous arms around Kate's waist and pulled her near. "I am pleasssssed you remember me."

No words came to Kate, but a powerful shiver ran through her whole body.

"You have assissssted me, whether you like it or not," said Nimue, speaking directly in Kate's ear. "Tell me, now. Am I correct that the old fool over there hassss brought me the Horn?"

"No!" cried Geoffrey. "Don't answer her!"

Kate tried to resist, but a powerful force made her speak. "Y-yes. He h-has it."

"Exccccellent."

Nimue uncoiled her arms, leaving Kate trembling. With a low laugh that rippled up and down her smokelike form, the enchantress floated over to the throne in the center of the great hall and settled into it. Resting her head against the throne's back, she lifted her dagger and began casually twirling it in her long black hair. Finally, she swung her gaze toward Garlon and addressed him as if the former sea captain were nothing but a lackey.

"You. Fetch me the prisonerssss."

Garlon winced, then turned and strode across the room to the cage. With a blazing sweep of the sword of light, he sliced through a row of bars. A hole opened in the cage and through it crawled Isabella and Jim.

Kate and her father ran to each other and embraced. The feel of his arms, so warm and strong, melted the lingering chill of Nimue's touch. A surge of hope, small but tenacious, began to rise inside her.

Garlon shoved Jim roughly. "Get going."

Kate separated from her father. Isabella took her arm as they walked past Nimue's throne to rejoin Geoffrey and Terry. The enchantress, still twirling her hair with the dagger, observed them. Then she spat out another command.

"Now fetch me the Horn."

Garlon advanced toward Geoffrey. Sword gleaming at his side, he ordered, "Give it to me."

Geoffrey tried to hold his bent body upright. "I'd rather not."

The sword of light lifted. "Give it to me, old man, before I smite you with this."

For several seconds, no one moved. A drop of perspiration rolled down Geoffrey's long nose, hovering at the very tip before falling into his beard. At last, he cleared his throat and uttered a single word.

"No."

Rage sparked in Garlon's eyes and he stepped closer. "One more time. Give it to me or I will take it."

His hands twitching at his side, Geoffrey stared defiantly at Garlon. Then, without warning, he spat in the ruffian's face.

"*Aaaargh!*" Garlon started to bring down the sword on Geoffrey's head.

"Sssstop," barked Nimue.

Garlon froze, his blade only inches from the white mane. He looked anxiously at the enchantress.

"You brainlessss bungler."

Garlon cringed, but held his tongue. He lowered the sword.

"I ssssee now that I musssst do it myssssself." With a gruesome grin, Nimue raised the blackened dagger, watching it glint with the fire of the flaming chariot. Almost casually, she pointed it at Geoffrey.

A bolt of white lightning exploded from the dagger and struck Geoffrey full force in the chest. The old man shrieked and flew backward, landing in a heap on the other side of the room.

"Geoffrey!" cried Kate, sprinting to him.

She grabbed his robe and shook him. Nothing. She listened for his breath, for his heartbeat. Nothing. She called out his name again, hoping for some sign of life. Nothing.

Tears welling in her eyes, she stroked his haggard head for the last time. Then she stood and faced Nimue.

"You killed him."

"Of coursssse," replied Nimue calmly. "And now you will bring me the Horn."

Kate stiffened. "I will not."

At that, Nimue lifted her hand not holding the dagger. No one but Kate saw the flash of ruby light from one of her fingers.

"Pleasssse reconsssssider. I assssked you to bring me the Horn."

Without willing herself to do so, Kate knelt by the body of her slain companion. Haltingly, she reached under the folds of his robe, slipped the coral necklace over his head, and removed the glistening Horn. As she stood, light shimmered across its curves.

Seeing the Horn, her father caught his breath. He watched, frozen in place, as Kate began walking with a mechanical gait toward the enthroned enchantress, sloshing her feet across the watery floor.

Without warning, he stepped in front of her, blocking her path. "Don't do it," he told her. "Don't give her the Horn."

Kate looked up at him. She wanted badly, so badly, to do as he wished. Yet another, stronger power commanded her to do otherwise. For a moment she hesitated, then continued walking straight ahead, as though her father did not exist.

As she bumped up against him, he gazed at her, dumbfounded. "What's the matter with you, Kate? I told you to stop."

"And I told her to come," replied Nimue, giving another low, guttural laugh. "Now you can ssssee where your daughter'ssss true loyalty liessss."

Jim tried to seize the Horn from her hands, but she dodged him. Whirling to face Nimue, he shouted, "What have you done to her?"

"Sssso," hissed the enchantress. "The protective father returnssss. Or issss it the greedy father, who would like the Horn all to himsssself? One never knowssss." She waved one of her smoky fingers at Garlon. "Go to him, will you? But do not ssssmite him until I ssssay."

Garlon bounded to Jim's side and held the sword of light at his chest.

Kate, still holding the Horn, shook herself. "Wait!" she called to Nimue, speaking groggily. "You promised . . . promised you would . . . not harm him."

Nimue twirled her hair relaxedly for a while. "Yessss, I ssssuppose I did." She peered at Kate. "But it doessss not matter, ssssince I have a better idea."

The enchantress coiled the lower part of herself around the arm of the throne, basking in the heat of the flaming chariot. "Garlon," she instructed, "I want you to take the Horn from the girl. But do not take a drink for yoursssself! Not until I ssssay. Or what happened to that old fool will happen to you."

His hand quivering with excitement, Garlon snatched the Horn from Kate, all the while keeping his sword aimed at Jim. He brought the prize toward his face, then lowered it when he heard Nimue hiss angrily.

"Now Garlon," commanded Nimue. "Give the ssssword of light to the girl."

The seaman's jaw dropped. "Give her what?"

"The ssssword of light." Speaking to Kate, she declared, "I want you to hold the ssssword, but harm no one."

Kate nodded, as Garlon hesitantly gave her the weapon.

Grasping the hilt with both hands, she could feel it vibrating with energy. The thought half formed in her mind to strike down both Garlon and Nimue, but it was swiftly overpowered by a desire to do exactly as the enchantress had commanded. She stood as still as stone, holding the bright sword.

"Exccccellent. Now we shall tesssst both the sssstrength of your will and the sssstrength of my ring." Nimue purred with delight before issuing her next order. "I want you to raisssse the ssssword above your head."

Kate did as she said.

"And now . . . I want you to kill your father."

A jolt of revulsion struck Kate. Yet, despite everything she felt, she found herself bracing to bring down the sword. She could hear the cries of Isabella and Terry, could see the horror in her father's face, could feel her stomach churning in torment. *I can't,* she told herself with great effort. *I can't do it.*

Even so, her hands tightened around the hilt, preparing to deal a powerful blow. Then, dimly at first, another idea surfaced in her mind.

"You . . . promised you wouldn't . . . harm him."

Nimue grinned broadly. "Yessss, but I made no promisssse about what *you* might do."

Kate shuddered, fighting back the power of Nimue's desire. *I can't. I w-w-wo . . .* She tried with all her concentration to say the word. *Won't. I won't.*

She lowered the sword ever so slightly, feeling stronger by the second. *I won't.* Shaking with strain, she began to take control of herself once more.

Nimue thrust out her hand. The ring flashed ruby red, blinding Kate's vision and assaulting her will.

"I sssssaid, kill your father."

"But—"

"Kill your father."

Kate looked from the void of Nimue's eyes to the terror of her father's. The stench of vomit seared her throat. Perspiration stung her eyes.

At that instant, a sudden trembling shook the floor of the great hall. Kate caught sight of the pile of brown rags that once was Geoffrey. His robe seemed to flutter in a wind that she could not feel. As she watched, the edges of his garment began to glitter, as if touched by the rays of a distant sunrise.

Then, miraculously, the robe deepened in color to azure blue, while silvery stars and planets sprouted along its borders. Geoffrey himself sat up with a start, even as his body began to transform. As he rose to his feet he grew markedly broader, until he was almost as stout and square-shouldered as Garlon. The hair on his head and beard lengthened and developed flecks of red amidst the white. The curve of his cheekbones lifted, and his hawklike nose twisted and developed a hairy wart on one side. Wrinkles far deeper than Geoffrey's lined his brow, although the coal black eyes remained the same.

Nimue released a long, shrill hiss but remained motionless.

The man raised his prominent eyebrows, and a brief blast of wind knocked the sword of light from Kate's hands. As it slapped the coursing surface of the floor, she staggered backward. For the first time since seeing Nimue again, she felt like her own self.

"Merlin," she whispered, astonished. She traded glances with her father.

"Oldest at birth, youngest at death," quoted Jim, studying the wizard's profile like a piece of long-lost parchment.

Without taking his eyes off Nimue, Merlin spoke to the

historian in a resonant voice. "An exceptional ballad, that. My only regret was that Saint Godric never got around to arranging it for troubadours."

Garlon started to speak, but choked on the words. He took a small step backward, cradling the Horn in his arms.

Merlin bowed slightly, still watching the throne. "It has been a long time, brother." His voice echoed in the chamber.

"I thought, I thought you were dead," stammered Garlon.

"You and many others." His jaw clenched. "Do you regret your treachery?"

"No! You brought it on yourself, by thinking you were so much better than everyone else."

Merlin's eyes bored into his brother's. "I have made my mistakes, just like you. I have paid a hefty price, just like you. Now I ask you, can you look to the future and not to the past? Can you cast aside petty jealousy and take my hand?"

Garlon grimaced. "Only to slice it off."

"Fool! You have not changed one bit! You were stupid to join the likes of Nimue."

"You are the stupid one if you think you can stop us now."

"I can stop you," answered Merlin. "I can stop you both."

"That," rasped the enchantress, "issss where you are wrong."

XXVII

CHECKMATE

It wassss clever of you to essssscape from the cave," declared Nimue, her vaporous arms slashing the air. "You dessssserve credit. But it will not change the outcome. It will merely ssssweeten my victory."

Merlin studied her with regret. "Once . . . you were so much more than this. You were . . . magnificent."

Nimue's face tightened.

"You valued knowledge more than power, beauty more than gain. I recall a time—was it so long ago?—when you turned the sands of a parched desert into a newborn sea, flowering with sea anemones. You even told me that sometimes you wished you had been born a sea anemone, so graceful and beautiful, so free from the tragedy and remorse that fill our lives."

"Ssssentimental fool! Who would want to be a lowly ssssea anemone, fixed to ssssome rock, unable to move, even when attacked by a sssslimy sssslug?" The enchantress coiled and uncoiled her vaporous arms. "I ssssee you have learned nothing from your yearssss of confinement."

"And what have you learned?"

"That I have only one dessssire, the Horn. You denied me it oncccce. You shall not again!"

With that, Nimue aimed her dagger straight at Merlin.

Just as a bolt of lightning burst from the blade, the wizard leaped away. The bolt missed him narrowly but grazed his beard, scorching several hairs. Merlin flew into Garlon, knocking him over and sending the Horn skidding across the wet floor.

Landing near the glassy table laden with Treasures, Merlin plucked one of his own hairs and touched it to the whetstone.

"Blade!" he cried.

Instantly, the hair sizzled and exploded in a cloud of smoke. In its place Merlin held a gleaming sword with the hilt cupped over his hand. Shaking the rapier at Nimue, he declared, "If it is fire you want, then fire you shall get."

He advanced toward the enchantress. Suddenly he stopped. His cape had caught on the corner of the table.

"Look out!" shouted Kate.

The wizard spun backward as another bolt of lightning crashed past, shattering the table to shards. Treasures sprayed in all directions. At the same time Garlon took up the sword of light and slashed at Merlin's head.

The two bright swords clashed, throwing sparks in all directions. Between thrusts and parries, Merlin glanced repeatedly at the Horn lying on the floor. Yet every time he attempted to edge closer to it, Garlon fought him off, trying to do the same.

The two burly men fought furiously, working their way around the burning chariot. Fire from the chariot as well as their swords leaped at their clothing. For a split second Kate lost sight of them behind a blast of orange flames. Then Merlin reappeared, running to fetch the Horn.

But Nimue, seeing her opportunity, moved faster. Trails of mist flowing behind, she lifted off the throne and flew toward the shell-shaped Treasure.

In desperation, Merlin threw his sword like a lance at the Horn. It struck its target full force, sending the Horn sliding toward Jim.

"Throw it to me!" called Merlin.

Jim gathered up the Horn and started to hurl it to Merlin, when he abruptly caught himself. Gazing with wonder at the shimmering object, he held it before his face. All at once he seemed overcome with desire, and lifted the Horn to take a drink.

"Throw it!" Merlin cried.

Isabella tugged on Jim's arm. "Come on, throw it!"

Jim hesitated, giving Nimue just enough time to pluck the Horn from his grasp. With a savage swipe of her arm, she knocked him backward. Then she announced, "I shall be the one to tasssste itssss power."

"No!" bellowed Merlin, charging at her.

Just then Garlon careened around the chariot and collided into Nimue. The Horn flew into the air, bounced off the throne, and rolled to a far corner of the room.

"Sssstupid fool," cursed the enchantress, starting after the Horn.

Merlin changed course, hoping to get there first. But Garlon, seeing him, wheeled around and intercepted him. Panting, he prepared to strike down his brother with the sword of light.

"Garlon," pleaded Kate. "Don't!"

"I've got you now," crowed the seaman, swinging his weapon.

Merlin drew a quick breath, then lunged—not at Garlon, but at the chessboard sitting on the arm of the throne. He grabbed one of the wooden chess pieces and tumbled aside, chanting, "Arise now. Arise!"

Nothing happened. Merlin closed his eyes and squeezed the chess piece in his fist. Garlon, sensing his opportunity, advanced boldly. Across the room, Nimue raced toward the Horn.

Kate anxiously asked her father, "What was the chessboard supposed to do?"

"The pieces," he replied, "were able to—"

Just then, a series of loud reports filled the great hall. The chess pieces suddenly swelled to enormous size. Thirty-two stern figures, each one twice as tall as a man, surrounded the throne, motionless as statues. Beside Merlin, a red knight with the head of a huge horse stood glowering at Garlon.

"Come alive," finished Jim, awestruck.

Merlin regained his feet and raised his eyes to the towering knight. Then he turned to Garlon and declared, "I shall be red."

In response, Garlon pointed to a black knight of equal size. "I shall be black."

As if on cue, the two knights reared back, whinnied and charged headlong into each other. They crashed together with such impact that they flew backward, skidding across the slippery floor. The black knight plowed into Nimue before she could reach the Horn. Enraged, Nimue spat out a curse that sent him flying right into the flaming chariot. As fire devoured his wooden body, shrieks of pain echoed among the arches.

Giant chess pieces all around joined in the fray. They collided into one another and slammed into arches and walls. Hammering and pounding, they attacked one another fiercely.

Garlon mounted another black knight and rode into combat. Brandishing the sword of light, he chopped mercilessly at two red pawns and a rook. He had nearly gained the upper hand when Nimue, who was being pursued by a pair of huge bishops, yanked the sword from him, leaving him to fend for himself.

Meanwhile, as Merlin retrieved his own sword, a black rook charged full speed at him, intent on running him down. A split second before the collision, the red queen cast herself in the rook's path, bowling him over sideways.

In gratitude, Merlin turned to the red queen, bowed, and said, "Lovely move."

The queen curtsied, then replied, "Queen takes rook. One of my best."

Kate turned to her father. "In chess, if you knock out the other side's king . . . don't you win?"

His eyes ignited. "It's worth a try."

The two of them plunged into the battle, dodging several chess pieces until they found the enemy king. As the king bent to catch them, they started running circles around him until the giant warrior started to teeter dizzily. Then, in unison, they hurled themselves bodily at him. He fell over with a crash.

Swiftly, Kate and her father rolled the king through a gaping hole that had opened in the wall. As they heard the splash below, all the other black chess pieces instantly froze in place, unable to move.

"We won!"

Kate's cry was joined by the cheers of the red chess pieces, as well as Jim, Terry, and Isabella.

At that moment, Merlin spied a cloud of dark vapor drawing near to the Horn. "Stop her," he shouted above the din. "Before she gets it!"

Terry, who was standing near the Horn, scooped it up, even as Nimue bore down on him. He threw it to Merlin.

"I have it!" trumpeted the wizard, holding the Horn above his head.

In a flash, Nimue changed tactics. Instead of flinging herself at Merlin, she braced her wispy form and pointed the sword of light straight at the fiery chariot.

"Checkmate!" she cried, as a violent tremor rattled the great hall. A seething, thundering roar, coming from far below the castle's foundations, swelled to deafening volume. The Glass House rocked so wildly that everyone, including Nimue, tumbled to the floor. Merlin pitched to one side, dropping the Horn, while the chariot spouted flames all the way to the vaulted ceiling.

The crystal throne fell on its back, splitting in two. Scorched by the blazing chariot, its once-transparent frame turned to blackened coals. As the fire burned hotter, the throne melted into a simmering puddle, then began to evaporate. Soon not a trace of it remained.

As Kate labored to regain her feet, another convulsion hit. More powerful than the first, it did not merely bend the castle walls. It broke them, burst them, splitting apart the flowing beams and buttresses. The force of the tremor hurled Kate like a missile into the cauldron of knowledge, which teetered briefly then fell to the floor with a resounding thud.

"The cauldron," called Merlin from across the room. "Set it right again!"

Before Kate could do anything, however, a deep crack opened in the aqueous floor. All the bubbling yellow liquid in the cauldron poured out and vanished down the dark fissure. All, that is, but a single drop, which spattered onto her wrist, stinging like a dart.

At once, an idea dawned in her mind. Spotting the copper-red mantle lying next to a fallen column, she crawled hurriedly toward it. From the edge of her eye she saw Merlin and Nimue attack each other with renewed ferocity. Between them, lying on the floor, rested the Horn. Their clashing swords rang out, barely audible above the tumult of the castle collapsing around them.

Grasping the mantle, Kate flung it over her shoulder like a cloak. It smelled of dried autumn leaves and rustled noisily. She started to buckle its golden clasps, when her hands disappeared before her face. *Invisible,* she said to herself in disbelief. *I'm invisible.*

Struggling to keep her balance, she did her best to dash across the vibrating hall to the place where Merlin and Nimue battled. As she approached, the wizard lost his footing and lurched to the floor. Nimue, seizing the advantage, bent to retrieve the Horn. At the same time, Kate hurled herself at it. Barely an instant before the hand of the enchantress closed on the spot, Kate grabbed the Horn and spun away.

Nimue froze. "The Horn," she rasped. "It dissssappeared!"

Merlin, looking equally perplexed, clambered to his feet. Then a strange light flickered in his eyes. He backed away, in the direction of the chariot, taunting Nimue to follow him.

Simultaneously, Kate stood, holding the Horn. She could see her father and Isabella running to escape from a toppling column. As the column smashed to bits behind them, she cried out.

Hearing her voice, Jim stopped abruptly, followed by Isabella. "Kate," he called. "Where are you?"

"Here," she shouted back. Then, remembering her invisibility, she tore off the mantle. "Right here!"

"I see you now," he answered. "Let's get out of here before—"

A great crack appeared, snaking across the floor with dreadful speed. It cut directly beneath the feet of Jim and Isabella, widening into a chasm. As Kate watched helplessly, it swallowed them whole.

"No!" she screamed as they dropped out of sight. She sprinted toward the chasm, but before she reached the edge a strong hand grabbed her by the chin and wrenched her down. The Horn fell from her grasp.

Garlon stood above her, frowning. Without a word, he lifted his sword to kill her.

Suddenly a figure jumped Garlon in a flying tackle. The seaman stumbled, twisting violently under the weight of his assailant.

"Leave her alone," ordered the man clinging to his back.

"Terry!" cried Kate, pushing to her feet.

She had barely spoken his name when Garlon jerked forward, throwing Terry to the floor. Garlon swung the sword, but Terry deftly dodged the blow and grabbed him by the ankle. As Garlon fell, Terry pounced on top of him. The two men grappled, rolling one on top of the other.

Kate stood by helplessly, not knowing what to do. She had no weapon, but even if she had one, how could she use it against Garlon without injuring Terry?

They rolled to the very edge of the chasm, fighting to control the sword. Bloodstains streaked their arms and legs as well as the slick floor. Terry's youth and added weight seemed an equal match for Garlon's brawn and experience, for every time one gained an advantage, the other would reverse it.

At length Garlon kicked Terry off of him. He stumbled to his feet, grasping the sword, then raised it wrathfully. Terry lay on his back, helpless, as the sea captain reared back to strike.

Suddenly Garlon pitched backward as one foot slipped into the chasm. An expression of horror on his face, he swung the sword frantically to keep his balance.

"He's going to fall!" cried Kate.

Then, even as he tumbled over the edge, he whipped his arm and threw the sword straight into Terry's chest. With a cry of anguish that mingled with his victim's, Garlon the Seaworthy plunged into the dark waters below.

Kate ran to Terry's side and pulled out the sword. He groaned as blood spurted from the wound.

Laying a hand on his forehead, she looked around frantically for Merlin. For help. But Merlin was nowhere to be found. All she could see was the collapsing castle and the inferno in the center of the great hall.

She turned back to Terry. He squinted up at her, trying to form some words with his lips.

"Don't talk," she whispered.

He grimaced, then forced himself to speak. "This time . . . I tried."

Her eyes clouded. Now it was she who could not speak. She felt his body grow relaxed and still.

Slowly, she stood, her heart aching. She had lost everyone. Dad, who loved her no less than she loved him. Isabella, who showed her the stars in a single drop of seawater. And now Terry, who mattered more than she would ever have guessed. She shuffled aimlessly toward the flaming chariot, half hoping that another chasm would open up and swallow her, too.

Then she saw an enormous chunk of the ceiling break loose and smash to the floor on the other side of the chariot. Along with the impact, however, she heard familiar voices shriek in pain.

She sprinted to the spot. There she found both Merlin and Nimue, pinned beneath the weighty chunk, which was sliding into a large hole in the floor. The head of the enchantress and the chest of the wizard were held completely immobile. Meanwhile, their arms groped madly for the sword of light, which lay just beyond their reach. In a matter of seconds, the chunk would tumble into the chasm, taking both of them with it.

Crawling as near as she dared, Kate grasped the sword of light. She started to hand it to Merlin, who was struggling so hard he had not yet seen her, when suddenly a ruby light flashed in her eyes.

"Give the ssssword to me," hissed a voice.

She jerked back her hand holding the sword. Hesitantly, she began to reach not toward Merlin but toward the thin, vaporous arm that beckoned to her.

"Closssser. Come closssser."

She stretched to give the sword to Nimue, even as the chunk slid deeper into the hole, dragging down the enchantress. Farther Kate reached, and farther.

Then, as Nimue's fingers nearly closed on the hilt, Kate caught a glimpse of the bottomless eyes. For a fraction of a second, she recoiled. *Nimue! I'm saving Nimue.*

"Closssser! You are wassssting time."

Hesitantly, Kate moved nearer. Her stomach knotted. *Nimue . . . those eyes. Those horrible eyes! I ca . . . can't.*

The ruby light flashed again, blinding her. But unlike before, she fought to see through it, to see with her own eyes.

"Give it to me," ordered Nimue, sounding desperate. *"Give it to me now."*

"No," said Kate aloud. In that instant, she swept her arm toward Merlin and placed the sword of light in his hand.

The wizard, seeing her at last, grabbed the sword and immediately started hacking away at the heavy chunk, even as it dropped lower. Finally he freed himself and crawled to safety.

Seething with rage, he pointed the sword of light at Nimue. He readied to run her through, knowing the powerful weapon would destroy her. Then, to Kate's surprise, he hesitated.

Nimue eyed him savagely. "You ssssentimental fool! Kill me while you have the chancccce."

"No," said Merlin. He flung the sword aside. "I will do better."

The anger melted from his face, replaced with steely calm. He raised his hand and pointed a single outstretched finger at the enchantress.

In a flash, Nimue vanished. In her place lay a simple sea anemone, its black tentacles as long and flowing as her hair had once been. Fixed to a rock, unable to move, it was swept downward into the chasm as the chunk gave way completely.

No sign of Nimue remained, not even a scream.

XXVIII
UNENDING SPIRAL

Holding tight to Kate's wrist, Merlin pulled her away from the hole. His cape torn, his hair disheveled, he looked more like Geoffrey than the great wizard.

He gazed at her solemnly before speaking. "You resisted the ring. That took enormous strength of will, enough to break Nimue's hold on you. I am grateful."

She bowed her head. "It won't bring back my dad, though. Or the others."

Placing his hand upon her shoulder, he said, "You did your best."

"It wasn't enough."

"It was enough to keep the Horn from Nimue." Merlin then turned and walked, a bit shakily, past the flaming chariot to what remained of the throne of Merwas. There, amidst the rubble, rested the Horn itself. He carefully picked it up, watching it reflect the firelight. Then he said, with the sadness of centuries, "I have lost so much, so very much. But once again, for a brief moment at least, I hold you, Serilliant."

And he recited:

Never doubt the spiral Horn
Holds a power newly born,
Holds a power truly great,
Holds a power ye create.

He pivoted to face Kate. "It may make little difference to you now, but you are, from this day forward, a member of the Order of the Horn."

"This day is probably my last," she said somberly.

"All the more important, then, that you receive your due." He offered her the Horn of Merlin. "Drink."

"Me?" she sputtered.

He slipped the coral necklace over her head. "Merwas decreed, *Only those whose wisdom and strength of will are beyond question may drink from this Horn.*"

"I—I don't know if I should."

"Perhaps you would like first to smell its special fragrance. Then you can better decide whether you want to drink."

Hesitantly, Kate lifted the Horn's gleaming rim to her nose. She sniffed gingerly at first, then closed her eyes and inhaled deeply.

Strange sensations swirled through her. A meadowlark singing. A book opening. First morning light. Tasting fresh melon, tart and tangy. Joining hands! Pearls of dew in a lupine leaf. A winged creature, emerging from its cocoon. Warm hearth. Cold lemonade. A baby colt, struggling to stand. An infant garbling his first words. Practicing piano, finally getting it right. Tossing the pitch, starting the game. Subtle sunrise, setting fire to fields of snow. Fresh water, chilling tongue and teeth. Diving in, *splash!* Blueberry muffins, still steaming, oozing butter. A first kiss. An inspiration. A young sapling, shading the stump of a fallen elder. Shooting stars. A dream to start the day. And, underlying all, the fragrant air of the mountaintop.

Kate opened her eyes.

"Well?"

"It's . . . wonderful."

A spare smile appeared on Merlin's face. "Drinking will be even better."

"I have the feeling that, when I take a drink, it will be as if my life is . . . starting over somehow."

"Easier said than done," cautioned the wizard. "But, yes, that's the idea. After you drink, your grief will be no less than before. But your ability to make choices may be a bit greater. And if you can choose, you can create."

Kate looked again at the gleaming Treasure. A magical Horn, a whirlpool, a strand of DNA. It seemed right that they should all possess the same spiral shape. She pondered Merlin's words. *If you can choose, you can create.* In a way, creation itself was shaped like a spiral. A vast, continuing, unending spiral.

She moved a step nearer. "I think I understand."

Merlin trained his eyes on her. "Understand what?"

"The power of the Horn. It's not about living forever, stretching your life on and on like a rubber band. It's about living *young*. Starting your life over, all the time."

Showing no expression, Merlin said, "Go on."

"That's why the ship, the fish, the whirlpool, even Geoffrey—I mean you—all stay so young." She twirled her braid, thinking. "It's almost like a kind of . . . creation. The power to create your own life, to make new choices, to begin again."

"Serilliant. Beginning." Merlin gazed into the curling Horn. "The Emperor Merwas knew that renewed life is the most precious kind of eternal life. For despite all the sorrows and losses of living, each new day is freshly born."

Then the wizard gestured at the once-magnificent castle. "Come now. Take your drink, while you still can."

Feeling the pull of the Horn's power, Kate pursed her lips to take her first swallow. But even as she smelled its fragrance again, something made her stop.

The power to create your own life . . . She remembered being a water spirit, so full of possibilities. How had Isabella put it? *All the future lies within the present.* She remembered that every cell in her body can replace itself over time. And she remembered Nimue's ring, which would not let her make choices, would not let her be human.

She lowered the Horn.

Merlin scrutinized her. "You don't want to drink?"

"No. Not exactly. I don't *need* to drink." Seeing his puzzlement, she fumbled for some way to explain. "I, well, I don't really need the power . . . from somewhere else. I . . . already have it."

Merlin observed her, as he played with his beard. "Wise you are, Kate. Drinking from the Horn will renew your body, but not necessarily your soul. That part is up to you. And you possess that power, here and now." Somberly, he reflected for a moment. "But . . . tell me. Wouldn't you like to live forever?"

"Sure I would. But even more, I guess, I'd like to grow. And change. Maybe the Horn, by making your body stop growing old, makes it easy to stop growing in other ways, too. Like . . . Nimue. Or Garlon. Or the whales."

The wizard nodded sadly. "I feel for the whales. Their pain is as great as the ocean itself! They need something more, something beyond the power of the Horn to provide.

They need . . . hope. That is my wish for them. It might come from any number of sources, even something as small as an isolated act of kindness. Or it might never come at all. Time will tell."

Hearing his voice, so much like Geoffrey's, Kate could not resist asking a question. "All that time you were in the whirlpool, did you look like yourself or like Geoffrey?"

"Like Geoffrey, to be sure! The last thing I wanted to do was to alert Nimue that Merlin had returned. That is why, when I finally escaped from the cave, I arranged the elaborate ruse of smuggling myself on board the *Resurrección*. The ship, I knew, would pass near the whirlpool. So after ensuring the sailors would be saved by the whales, I sank down to the bottom—hoping, perhaps, that someday a friend of Arthur's cause might find my clue on the ship's manifest and follow me."

Despite herself, Kate blushed.

Merlin straightened up proudly. "All Nimue ever suspected was that a bumbling old monk had been sucked down the whirlpool. Knowing that she watched me constantly, I remained disguised as Geoffrey so she wouldn't get alarmed and try something . . . drastic. As it was, she ran out of patience before I expected."

Kate cringed as a chunk of the ceiling slammed to the floor, spraying her with water. "So for all those years she couldn't get in, and you couldn't get out."

"Not until you gave me the idea." He smacked his lips as if remembering something tasty. "Fortunately, the ship was loaded with a good supply of . . . necessities."

"As well as your little red book."

At that moment, another tremor tore at the castle, ripping away an entire wall so that the gleaming stars of the cavern shone down on them directly. Kate, like Merlin, barely kept her balance. As the tremor subsided, she drank in the sight of the stars.

She thought of the world above the waves she would not see again. Of the people whose voices she would not hear again. Viewing the chasm where her father and Isabella had disappeared, not far from Terry's bloody body, she shook her head. "I only wish your little red book had some way to bring the dead back to life."

Merlin started. "How stupid of me!"

Before she could ask what he was doing, he pawed through some rubble and snatched up the knife that had rested on the glassy table. Then he ran to Terry's side and bent low. Ever so gently, he touched its tip to the wound in Terry's chest.

"The knife that can heal any wound!" exclaimed Kate, comprehending at last.

"It may be too late to help," warned Merlin. "If he has but a flicker of life still within him, the knife may revive him. But if he is gone, there is nothing more I can do."

Kate watched Terry's face for any sign of life, but saw none. "How long," she asked hoarsely, "before we know?"

"It may take some time." His expression grave, he added, "More time than we have left." With his free hand he scratched the point of his nose in the way Geoffrey often did. Then he declared, "Escape is still possible."

Dumbfounded, she scanned the crumbling walls of the castle. "Escape?"

"Before the eruption. But you must hurry! I would guess it is only seconds away."

"What do we do about Terry?"

"I will stay with him."

She realized that he meant her to go alone. "Forget it. I'm not going anywhere without you."

"You must," the wizard insisted. "And take with you the Horn." He glanced toward the shattered table of Treasures. "I would like to go with you. *Benedicite*, I would. But I cannot. Whether or not I can heal this young man, I might yet be able to find some way to shield the Treasures from being completely destroyed. If Arthur is ever to return, he will need them."

She turned the Horn in her hand. "But this is one of the Treasures, too."

Merlin shook his white head. "That may be true, but I have learned one thing in finding it, losing it, and finding it again. The Horn Serilliant deserves a life of its own. Its power is too great to be locked away, hidden from all the world. If it is to be one of Arthur's Treasures, then Arthur must one day find it himself."

"It should be kept somewhere safe. So someone like Nimue—or her sea demons—doesn't get it."

"It should go with you."

She looked from the Horn to Terry's still-motionless body. "I'm not leaving without you!"

Merlin gazed at her soulfully. "You must try to save yourself. That is what your father would want." He lowered his eyes. "And what I want."

"No."

"I will miss you, Kate Gordon."

"But I wouldn't have any idea what to do with the Horn!"

A low rumble shook the floor, almost drowning out Merlin's reply. "It is up to you to choose its rightful home."

He reached, it seemed, to touch her cheek, but never did. A jagged hole opened in the floor beneath her. She dropped into darkness.

XXIX
THE JAWS OF DEATH

With a splash, she plunged into the water.

The lake felt both warmer and darker than before. It stung her eyes. Murky spirals of sediment swirled around her like miniature maelstroms. Fighting her way back up, she wished she could still swim like a fish, moving with her spine instead of her limbs, breathing with gills instead of lungs, craving only water instead of air.

Bursting above the surface, she gasped for breath. The air reeked of sulphur, burning her throat. Clouds of mist obscured any view of the castle, let alone the starry cavern. Rumbling surrounded her, growing louder by the second, punctuated by the sound of the castle collapsing. Every few seconds, pieces of its structure dropped into the lake.

She wondered whether she would die by drowning or by boiling in the lava that she knew would soon spew forth, turning this undersea lake into a pot of boiling stew. *I'd rather drown*, she thought dismally. *It's quicker.*

A sudden chill gripped her. Like an eclipse passing over the sun, the chill extinguished her own light and warmth. She shivered, doubly so, for she knew what had caused the change. And she knew that there was one way to die even worse than boiling in lava.

She whirled around to face the sea demon.

Murderous teeth exposed, the huge sea demon drew nearer. Slithering through the water, it approached steadily, but relaxedly, as if savoring its moment of final revenge.

The Horn. It wants the Horn. Anger flared inside her, pushing back the chill. The Horn belonged to the world, as Merlin had said. Not to a demon.

She flipped a splash of water. "Try and get it," she taunted. "Just try."

The sea demon halted its advance, a look of sudden doubt on its face. Kate thought at first that her spurt of defiance had worked. Then she realized that another creature, even larger than the sea demon, was approaching from the opposite side.

Spinning her head, she found herself staring straight into a massive face. A face she had seen only once before, at equally close range.

It was the face of a whale.

The great creature spouted, spraying her with humid breath. Abruptly, he rolled to one side, sending a wave washing over her and his own barnacled back. Waving his pectoral fins aggressively, he made a sharp clicking that echoed and reechoed in the underwater cavern.

Great, thought Kate, blinking the stinging salt from her eyes. *A sea demon on one side, an angry whale on the other.*

Then the whale fell still. He watched her intently, his round eye not wavering. Although Kate could not be sure, he seemed to regard her with something other than malice. Something more like . . . recognition.

At that moment the sea demon released a deep, fierce growl. She felt cold again, colder than before. She turned to see the sea demon swimming toward her again.

Another wave rolled over her as the whale, bending his enormous back, dived into the lake. As he submerged, he raised his tail high into the air—a tail whose fluke had been recently severed.

Kate bit her lip, as a rush of memory flooded her. She saw once more the helpless animal, golden in the moonlight, struggling to stay alive. She heard his mournful cry of death, felt his flailing tail. *So he did survive, after all.*

Facing the sea demon once more, her brief sense of celebration vanished as quickly as it had appeared. Worse, she could no longer summon her courage, or even her anger. All she felt was fear. Fear as cold and deep as the eyes of Nimue.

Fast approaching, the sea demon growled vengefully. Its immense jaws opened, ready to devour its prey and claim its prize.

At that instant, a wave lifted around Kate. Then she realized with a shock that it was no wave. A gigantic mouth rose above the surface, and she was in its center. As swiftly as it carried her upward, the mouth closed around her.

Everything went black.

Her first impulse was to fight. Against the lack of light and air, against the fringes of baleen that pushed at her from all sides, against the fear of being eaten alive.

Futilely, she struggled. Countless rows of baleen, like the bristles of vast brushes, pressed tightly against her. She could hardly move, hardly breathe. She had been swallowed, like Jonah. Swallowed by a whale.

Then, all at once, it came clear. Like the sailors of an ancient ship, she was being borne by a whale who wanted to save her. Yet this time no land was near. And this time something else would pursue them. She ceased struggling, working her way into a small pocket of air above the whale's tongue. For now, at least, she could breathe, though the air stank of undigested krill. Her feeling of dread only deepened.

The whale's angle changed sharply from vertical to horizontal. He dropped back to the water with a loud splash. In another instant he was diving again, bearing his human passenger.

A desperate race ensued, one that Kate could see only in her mind's eye. Beyond the powerful thumping of the whale's heart, beyond the constant whipping of his tail, she could hear the enraged growling of the sea demon, and beyond that, the ever-increasing rumble of the impending eruption.

For minutes that seemed like hours, the whale sped onward, swimming on a level keel. Then, unmistakably, the growling drew nearer, even as the chill in Kate's bones grew stronger. A wrenching turn threw her hard against the whale's jaws. The growling receded slightly.

The whale raced through the depths. More and more often, the pumping of his tail would slow for several strokes before speeding up again. Kate could almost feel his growing exhaustion. She wondered how long he could keep this up, how long before the sea demon's own jaws would tear into them both.

She tried to picture where they might be, recalling visions of the cavern, the coral jungle, the undersea stars, the ruins of the watery castle. All the while, the volcanic rumbling around them swelled louder.

All of a sudden, the whale veered upward. Kate slid further down his titanic tongue, moist and reeking of krill. She realized they must be climbing back up through the abyss. She could only hope that no spiderlike monster would be waiting for them at the entrance. To the rear, the sea demon's growling grew louder. Faster and faster beat the heart of the whale. Faster and faster beat Kate's own.

Was he going to try to carry her all the way to the surface? Even if they made it, how could they possibly stop the sea demon from getting them as well as the Horn? Fears rolled through her mind, one following the next, like waves on the beach.

Then came a new fear, more potent than all the rest. Her air was running out! She gasped, or tried to gasp. Panic seared her brain. She needed more air, needed it *now*. She could not breathe!

Her head started throbbing. Silently, she screamed. Her limbs and chest began to go numb. A shadow darkened her consciousness, made it hard to think. Hard to remember. Anything.

The shadow consumed her. She lay still.

Her head drooped a little, only as much as the fringes of baleen would allow. Yet that was just enough to bring her face near the curling Horn hanging from her neck.

The fragrance, the feeling, surged through her once more. She opened her eyes. She breathed again.

Her father's first description of Serilliant came back to her, as though he were speaking right in her ear. *Emrys endowed it with a virtue. Anyone who held it near could smell the fragrant air of the mountaintop, even if he did so at the bottom of the sea.* She brought the Horn closer, inhaling gratefully.

With a lurch, the young whale swung sideways. He was swimming horizontally again, his tail working frantically. He was not heading for the surface after all. Where then was he going?

The rumbling rose to a crescendo. Though she could no longer hear the wrathful growling, she still could feel the creeping chill. She knew the sea demon was almost on top of them.

The whale changed course again. Now he was turning in tighter and tighter circles. He seemed to be spiraling downward. As though he were entering the whirling wall of . . .

In an ear-shattering blast, the sea floor erupted. The force of the explosion knocked the whale savagely, tossing him about like a tiny seed in a gale.

Then, with terrible suddenness, his jaws opened. Out spilled Kate.

XXX

AN UNEXPECTED TWIST

She landed, dizzy and disoriented, on a hard surface. She could feel the Horn, still tied around her neck.

Half stunned, she stretched out her arms. A wooden deck! Could it be? She sat bolt upright. Her eyes viewed the ragged sails, the iron cannons, the weblike rigging. Her lungs drank the misty, sulphurous air.

In the next instant, several things happened at once. Things that convinced her that she had indeed returned to the *Resurrección*, that she was indeed alive.

The ocean floor shuddered, heaved and broke apart. Streams of molten lava and superheated gases burst into the water, hissing and roaring like thousands of turbines. The *Resurrección* rocked and pitched as if caught in a ferocious storm, forcing her to cling to the rigging to keep from flying overboard.

At the same time, the whirlpool slowed dramatically and contracted, bringing the whirling wall within a few feet of the ship. Curtains of water rained down on the deck.

As the whirlpool contracted, Kate caught sight of a gray

streak circling in the vortex. The whale! Suddenly she understood the final few seconds of her wild ride. In those sharp, successive turns he had entered the whirlpool; in that downward spiral he had moved into its spinning core. Then, to keep her out of the sea demon's reach, the whale had hurled her onto the deck.

With a pang, she recalled Terry's prediction that no living creature could survive the whirlpool unless it slowed down significantly. She wished she could tell him that he had been right. And, with deeper regret, she thought of how much her father would have loved to see this very ship. Even lashed by such a raging storm. Even for an instant. Even if the slowing whirlpool would soon collapse on itself, drowning the ship and anyone aboard under an ocean of water.

Then she glimpsed, near to the whale in the spinning wall of water, the blurred, twisted form of the sea demon. The sight made her cringe. She had eluded those jaws, at least for now. But what of the whale, who had given his all for the small chance she might be spared? There was no way she could possibly help him. She could only clutch the rigging and watch, water pouring down on top of her.

At that moment a cluster of new shapes in the whirlpool caught her attention. She could not be sure what they were, or whether she had really seen them spin past. Yet they seemed to be there, grappling with the sea demon, where they had not been only a split second before. And the sea demon seemed to be locked in battle, lashing out at these strange creatures that combined the bodies of people with the bodies of fish.

An enormous wave struck the hull, pitching the ship to one side. Water flowed under the ship, dislodging it from the sandy bottom. Simultaneously, the whirlpool slowed substantially, and then—for the briefest fragment of a heart-beat—it stopped spinning altogether.

In that instant, time itself froze. The whirlpool did not move, the ship did not pitch, Kate did not breathe. Her only sensation was the certainty of imminent death.

Then, just before the sea came crashing down upon her, the whirlpool started rotating again. Yet this time, something was different. At first she could not pinpoint precisely what had changed.

In a flash she comprehended. The whirlpool was turning *in the opposite direction*. Wrenched by the force of the volcanic eruption, the whirlpool's torque had reversed itself.

More water flooded underneath the ship, surging, pushing, lifting. And then a strange phenomenon occurred.

The ship began to rise.

Like a corkscrew that reverses and lifts upward, the whirlpool twisted toward the sky rather than the ocean floor. Higher and higher it carried the ship, in a slow and stately spiral, climbing gradually to the surface.

Kate's heart leaped. Might she actually see land again? Might she actually bear Merlin's Horn to safety? She craned her neck to look at the swelling circle of light above. Pastel pink and gold painted the sky. A new day was dawning.

Without warning, a burly arm reached out and tore the Horn from her neck, snapping the coral necklace in two. She stared, aghast, refusing to believe what she saw.

"So," sneered Garlon, standing before her on the deck. "Did you think you could escape me that easily?"

"Give it back!" she demanded, releasing her hold on the rigging. "It doesn't belong to you."

The sea captain laughed raucously. "The Horn belongs to whoever has it! And I intend to keep it for a long, long time."

"Don't, please. King Arthur will—"

"Never see it!" He laughed again, wiping his nose on his shirt. "Nor will my brother, the great Merlin. He is the stupid one, after all! So stupid he won't even leave a castle that is falling in."

"Merlin's not stupid," retorted Kate. "He just cares about others."

"Better to be alive," answered Garlon. With that, he lifted the Treasure toward his face. He gazed at it in satisfaction, twirling it in his hands. He seemed captivated by the golden light playing on its surface, light that grew stronger with every turn of the spiraling ship.

Suddenly he lurched violently, tackled from behind. The Horn slipped from his grasp and skated across the deck, coming to rest by a case of cannonballs.

Kate rolled out of her tackle and crawled madly toward it. But Garlon grabbed her by the calf and yanked her backward. Raging, he picked her up and shook her as though she were a rag doll.

"I should have broken your neck long ago," he fumed.

Just then the first fragile ray of sunlight, reflected off the brass door latch to the captain's quarters, touched his brow. Though a more gentle blow could not be devised, it seemed to strike him like a hammer. He staggered under the impact.

Nimue's curse, realized Kate, though she could not tell whether Garlon had felt the effect of the curse or merely his fear of it.

Frantically, Garlon threw her to the deck and ran to the Horn. He snatched it up and brought it to his face, ready to drink.

XXXI

A Day Without Dawn

At that instant, the ship burst above the waves. It began to circle the rim of the whirlpool, buoyed by the water rising through the funnel.

Garlon's eyes, so like his brother's and yet so different, danced with victory. Even as he raised the Horn to his lips, he seemed poised to release a long-awaited cheer.

Then his face contorted in a spasm of uncertainty, evolving slowly into terror. He dropped the Horn as his body convulsed, falling to the deck. A subtle perfume of apple blossoms blew past. The ship's bell tolled one time, echoing eerily. Garlon looked at Kate in horror, started to cry out, then vanished into the salty air.

The dead will die . . . Kate recalled the final words of the ballad, as she stared at the spot.

She glanced toward the east. The orange sun had barely begun to peek over the horizon. She lifted herself to her feet, only to witness a staggering sight.

Drawn upward by the reversed spiral of the whirlpool, an enormous volume of water lifted like a great wall around the

Resurreccíon. This circular tsunami, spinning slowly along with the ship, raised itself to a great height. It blocked the ascending sun, covering Kate and her vessel in shadow.

For a long moment, the towering wall of water hung there, ringing the ancient ship. Kate felt sure it would collapse any second, smashing the galleon to splinters. And she hardly cared if it did, now that Garlon had been destroyed. For the briny air of the surface reminded her more of what she had lost than of what she had won.

Collapse it did, but gently, smoothly. The wall of water melted into the sea, while the whirlpool, its power spent at last, started to merge with the prevailing currents of the Pacific. As the volcanic rifts far below finally quieted, giving the ocean floor a new geography, the whirlpool itself came to rest, returning the ocean surface to its geography of old. In a matter of minutes, the waves grew calm.

Remolino de la Muerté was no more.

Kate scanned the expanse of water, deep green with flecks of gold, surrounding the ship. The sun, now well above the horizon, beamed down on her warmly. Yet, for her, this was a day without a dawn, a day when the sun did not rise, either for her or for those she had lost beneath the waves.

No longer supported by the surging water of the whirlpool, the ship floated like a stick of driftwood, jostled by every wave. Kate reached for the Horn, lying near her on the deck. Again she studied its lustrous surface, its radiant liquid, its spiral design. And again she heard the voice of Merlin, saying, *It is up to you to choose its rightful home.*

But where could that be? Someplace safe, yet not completely hidden. Someplace where the enemies of Merlin and Arthur would not find it.

Maybe Merlin meant I should keep it myself. Strangely

tempted by the thought, she lifted the Horn, watching it shimmer in the sunlight. Perhaps she would change her mind and decide to drink from it one day. Or perhaps not. In any case, she would make a solemn promise to guard it for Arthur, to give it to him when he returned.

Or would she? In the presence of such power, would she eventually forget about her promise, as Merlin did long ago? And even if she could stay true, she was only one person. Those who craved the Horn would hunt for it relentlessly. She could not protect it from every conceivable threat.

Her mind drifted back to the story of the Horn. She thought of its many names, its many gifts, its many masters. She thought of its birth, inspired by the love of Emrys for Wintonwy. She thought of its connection to the mer people, ever elusive, and to the sea itself, the watery womb of all life.

As she stood on the deck of the ancient ship, an idea came to her. It was full of risk, yet it held a hint of hope. She looked into the Horn once more, then called out as loud as she could, "Serilliant!"

With that, she hurled it into the waves. For an instant it rested on the surface of the ocean. Then it sank out of sight.

She waited, watching, unsure what to expect.

At that moment, a ring of bubbles came to the surface, encircling the spot where the Horn had disappeared. Out of the sea rose a group of mer people, glistening green. In the middle of their circle, riding a low fountain of water, was the Horn of Merlin.

They had accepted her gift. With a single, soundless splash, they dived beneath the waves and disappeared.

Kate noticed that the *Resurrección* was listing more and more. No longer sustained by the power of the Horn, its timbers started to split and crack. A wave smashed the stern, throwing her into the rigging. The hull moaned like a living thing, then broke apart, its timbers dissolving into thousands of pieces. Into the ocean went the sails, the gold ingots, the jewels, the ivory combs, the cannons, the silks, and the thin red volume, all to be scattered on the bottom by the currents and tides.

Immersed in frigid water, Kate wrapped her arms around the remains of an old beam, hoping to stay afloat. She had no way of telling whether she would be carried out to sea, where she certainly would die, or back to the coast, where she would survive only if she could find a fishing village before falling prey to the desert sun.

A wave drenched her, nearly tearing her from the beam. Somehow she clung on. When she opened her eyes again, she saw a strange shape rising out of the ocean. She caught her breath.

The shape surged higher. At once she recognized it. She still could not breathe, though no longer out of fear. For there, moving toward her, was no sea demon, no phantom ship. It was the submersible.

The next several minutes flowed past as quickly as a crashing wave. The opening of the hatch. The shouts. The waves. The reunion she had never believed possible.

There was her father, hugging her so hard she thought her ribs would crack, then listening with care as she described her final moments with the Horn. There was Isabella, shaking with joy to see her, explaining how they had reached the submersible only seconds before the eruption, eager to hear about the young gray whale. There was the submersible, cramped but wholly satisfactory, bobbing where not long ago a great whirlpool had churned.

As Kate described Terry's gruesome fate, the others listened in disbelief.

"Can it be so?" asked Isabella, brushing back some stray hairs. "His life should not end that way."

Jim frowned. "No one's life should end that way."

In time, the conversation turned to other matters. Kate painted vivid portraits of her last encounters with Nimue, Garlon, and Merlin himself.

Her father looked at her affectionately. "You're not a bad storyteller, you know."

Despite her wet clothes, she felt a touch warmer. "It's in my genes."

"I can just hear you now," he predicted. "Sitting by the fire, surrounded by your grandchildren. One of them asks, 'Please, Granny, tell us the one about the battle of the giant chess pieces.'"

Kate joined in the laughter. "So I'll get to tell my own stories about Merlin." Then her expression changed. "Can you forgive me for almost following Nimue's orders?"

"If you can forgive me for following my own greed for the Horn. I found out down there that my motives were less pure than I had thought. Still . . . we did manage to prove the existence of Merlin, didn't we?"

"And not just in the sixth century."

"Right you are."

"He didn't look at all like what I expected."

"At least you got the wart on his nose right." He worked his tongue, pondering something. "I think you did the right thing with the Horn."

"You really think so?"

"I do. And if Merlin could be here with us, I'm sure he would, too."

She started to smile, then caught herself. "Maybe he *will* be with us again. And maybe he'll bring Terry back with him."

"I hope so," said her father.

"Do you think he can save him?"

"Merlin is capable of many things."

Isabella leaned closer. "As is *the place where the sea begins, the womb where the waters are born.*"

Jim gave her a nudge. "Not bad for a marine biologist."

Before Isabella could respond, a familiar wailing reached the submersible. Familiar, yet somehow changed. Hunched together, the trio listened to the creaking and moaning, clicking and whistling of the whales. They were all around, encircling the submersible, weaving their complex harmony.

"Something's different," said Jim after a while. "Do you hear it? Their singing isn't the same."

"Yes," answered Isabella. "There's a little less sadness."

Kate nodded, recalling Merlin's wish for the whales. "Or maybe . . . a little more hope."

Just then a gray whale, streams of water pouring from his body, launched out of the waves not far from the submersible. The whale paused, half in the water and half out, before falling back in a thunderous splash, spraying every window in the vessel.

Then he descended, lifting his severed tail into the air.

"That's him!" exclaimed Kate.

Isabella watched the whale submerge. "I have the feeling you two might meet again."

"Maybe."

"Hey," said Jim, "is anyone else hungry? I'm in the mood for a big helping of something. How about Baja Scramble?"

Isabella pouted. "I've been dreaming of pancakes."

"All right, then. We'll flip a coin."

"Here," announced Kate. "I've got one." She thrust her

hand into her pocket and pulled out a silver coin, as bright as if it had been freshly minted. A piece of eight.

The submersible pitched on the swells, as a lone gull screeched overhead. Waves slapped and surged, rocking to the rhythm of the sea.

THE BALLAD OF THE RESURRECCÍON

An ancient ship, the pride of Spain,
Embarked upon a quest
To navigate the ocean vast
And still survive the test.

It carried treasures rich and rare
Across the crashing waves
Beyond the flooded fields that are
So many sailors' graves.

Its goal to link the Orient
With distant Mexico,
The ship set sail with heavy hearts
And heavier cargo.

The galleon brimmed with precious gems,
Fine gold and silver wrought,
Silk tapestries and ivories
And spices dearly sought.

From China, Burma, Borneo,
Came crates of lofty cost,
And one thing more, the rumors said:
The Horn that Merlin lost.

Upon its prow, the words inscribed,
God bring us safe to land,
The ship at last raised all its sails
As lovers raised their hands.

Resurreccíon, O mighty ship,
You bear our very best!
Resurreccíon, O mighty ship,
Where will you come to rest?

Prevailing winds advancing east,
Pacific storms alive,
The brave men steered for Mexico
And prayed they might arrive.

They fought against the torrents,
A plague, a great typhoon,
Pursued by monsters of the deep
And pirates seeking boon.

The sailors suffered from the sun
That cracked and baked their skin,
Yet knew, between the sea and sun,
The sea would surely win.

For seven months they eastward sailed
Adrift upon the swells
Till even men whose hearts were strong
The stench of death could smell.

All water gone, as well as hope,
They grew too weak to stand
Until a voice cried loud and clear
"Land ho! I see the land!"

A joyous cheer arose that day
From sailors nearly dead,
Yet when they steered the ship to land
Their joy gave way to dread.

Resurreccíon, O mighty ship,
You bear our very best!
Resurreccíon, O mighty ship,
Where will you come to rest?

The ship began to list and spin
As sails apart did pull
And timbers buckled under waves
That smashed against the hull.

In circles tighter than a noose
The helpless vessel sailed
And every man upon the deck
Collapsed to knees and wailed.

For though the sea's a dangerous place
With terrors great and small,
Still mariners have always feared
The whirlpool most of all.

As swirling waters swamped the boat
And snapped a mast in two,
The galleon's mates leaped overboard
Into the churning blue.

The whirlpool dragged them under waves
Where endless chasms yawn.
The noble ship sank out of sight,
Its crew and cargo gone.

Then up from waters deep and dark
A pod of whales appeared.
They grabbed the men between their jaws
As Death's own jaws drew near.

Resurreccíon, O mighty ship,
You bear our very best!
Resurreccíon, O mighty ship,
Where will you come to rest?

To shore the saviors carried them,
And lo! The men survived.
They never knew why came the whales,
Nor why they were alive.

They only knew their ship was doomed
Because of Fate's cruel hand.
So many dreams and fortunes lost
Within the sight of land!

The whirlpool drowned the treasure ship
Upon that dreadful morn,
And buried it beneath the waves
Along with Merlin's Horn.

And so today the ship's at rest,
Removed from ocean gales,
Surrounded by a circle strange
Of ever-singing whales.

A prophesy clings to the ship
Like barnacles to wood.
Its origins remain unknown,
Its words not understood:

One day the sun will fail to rise,
The dead will die,
    And then
For Merlin's Horn to find its home,
The ship must sail again.